Hannah Cowley

The Runaway

A comedy

Hannah Cowley

The Runaway
A comedy

ISBN/EAN: 9783744743457

Printed in Europe, USA, Canada, Australia, Japan

Cover: Foto ©Andreas Hilbeck / pixelio.de

More available books at **www.hansebooks.com**

THE

RUNAWAY,

A

COMEDY:

As it is Acted at the

THEATRE-ROYAL

IN

DRURY-LANE.

LONDON:

Printed for the AUTHOR;

And Sold by Mr. DODSLEY, in Pall-Mall; Mr. BECKET, and Mr. CADELL, in the Strand; Mr. LONGMAN, in Pater-Noster-Row; and CARNAN and NEWBERY, in St. Paul's Church-Yard.

MDCCLXXVI.

T O

DAVID GARRICK, Efq;

S I R,

AMIDST the regrets I feel for your quitting the Stage, it is peculiarly gratifying, that a Play of *mine* clofes your *dramatic* life—It is the higheft pleafure to me, that *that* Play, from its fuccefs, reflects no difhonour on your judgement as a Manager.

Pofterity will know, thro' a thoufand Channels, that Mr. GARRICK was the ornament of the eighteenth Century, that he poffeffed the friendfhip of thofe whofe Names will be the glory of Englifh Hiftory, that the firft ranks in the kingdom courted his fociety—may my fmall voice be heard amongft thofe who will inform it, that Mr. GARRICK's *Heart* was no lefs an honour to him, than his *Talents!*

Unpatronized by any *name*, I prefented myfelf to you, obfcure and unknown. You perceived *dawnings* in my Comedy, which you *nourifh'd* and *improved*. With attention, and follicitude, you *embellifh'd*, and prefented it to the world—*that* World, which has emulated your generofity, and received it with an applaufe, which fills my heart with moft lively gratitude. I perceive how much of this applaufe I owe to my *Sex*.—The RUNAWAY has a thoufand faults, which, if written by a Man, would have incurred the fevereft lafh of Criticifm—but the Gallantry of the Englifh Nation is equal to its Wifdom—they beheld a *Woman* tracing with feeble steps the borders of the Parnaffian Mount——pitying her difficulties (for 'tis a thorny path) they gave their hands for her support, and placed her *high* above her level.

All this, Sir, and whatever may be its confequences, I owe to you. Had you rejected me, when I prefented my little RUNAWAY, depreffed by the refufal, and all confidence in *myfelf* deftroyed, I fhould never have prefumed to dip my pen again. It is now my task to convince You and the World, that a generous allowance for a young Writer's faults, is the beft encouragement to Genius—'tis a kindly Soil, in which weak Groundlings are nourifh'd, and from which the loftieft Trees draw their ftrength, and their beauty.

I take my leave of you, Sir, with the warmeft wifhes for your felicity, and Mrs. GARRICK's—to whofe *tafte,* and follicitude for me, I am highly indebted. May your recefs from the Stage be attended with all the bleffings of retirement and eafe—and may the world remember, in its moft diftant periods, that 'tis to Mr. GARRICK the Englifh Theatre owes its emancipation from groffnefs, and buffoonery—that to Mr. GARRICK's *Judgement* it is indebted for being the firft Stage in Europe, and to his *Talents* for being the delight of the moft enlightened and polifh'd age.

I am, Sir, your moft devoted,

and obedient humble Servant,

THE AUTHOR.

PROLOGUE.

Written by the AUTHOR.

Spoken by MR. BRERETON,

O The sweet prospect ! what a fine Parterre !
  Soft buds, sweet flowers, bright tints, and scented
    air !   [*Boxes.*
A Vale, where critic wit spontaneous grows !   [*Pit.*
A Hill, which *noise* and *folly* never knows ! [*Gallery.*
Let Cits point out green paddocks to their spouses ;
To me, no prospect like your crouded houses—
If, as just now, you wear those smiles enchanting;
But, when you frown, my heart you set a panting.
Pray then, for pity, do not frown to-night ;
I'll bribe—but how—Oh, now I've hit it—right.
Secrets are pleasant to each child of Eve ;
I've one in store, which for your smiles I'll give.
  O list ! a tale it is, not very common;
Our Poet of to-night, in faith's a—Woman,
A woman, too, untutor'd in the School,
Nor Aristotle knows, nor scarce a rule
By which fine writers fabricate their plays,
From sage Menander's, to these modern days :
How she could venture here I am astonish'd;
But 'twas in vain the Mad-cap I admonish'd ;
Told her of squeaking cat-calls, hisses, groans,
Off, offs, and ruthless Critics' damning moans.
I'm undismay'd, she cry'd, critics are Men,
And smile on folly from a Woman's pen :
Then 'tis the Ladies' cause, there I'm secure;
Let him who hisses, no soft Nymph endure;
May he who frowns, be frown'd on by his Goddess,
From Pearls, and Brussels Point, to Maids in Boddice.
  Now for a hint of her intended feast:
'Tis rural, playful,—harmless 'tis at least ;
Not over-stock'd with repartee or wit,
Tho' here and there *perchance* there is a hit ;

PROLOGUE,

For she ne'er play'd with bright Apollo's fire,
No Muse invok'd, or heard th' Aönian lyre;
Her Comic Muse—a little blue-ey'd maid,
With cheeks where innocence and health's display'd;
Her 'Pol—in petticoats—a romping Boy,
Whose taste is trap-ball, and a kite his joy:
Her Nursery the study, where she thought,
Fram'd fable, incident, surprise and plot.
From the surrounding hints she caught her plan,
Length'ning the chain from infancy to man:
Tom plagues poor Fan; she sobs, but loves him still;
Kate aims her wit at both, with roguish skill:
Our Painter mark'd those lines—which Nature drew,
Her fancy glow'd, and colour'd them—for you;
A Mother's pencil gave the light and shades,
A Mother's eye thro' each soft scene pervades;
Her Children rose before her flatter'd view,
Hope stretch'd the canvas, whilst her wishes drew.

We'll now present you drapery and features,
And warmly hope, you'll like the pretty creatures;
Then Tom shall have his kite, and Fan new dollies,
Till time matures them for *important* follies."

⁎ The dotted lines in the Play are omitted at the Theatre.

✻✻✻✻✻✻✻✻✻✻✻✻✻✻✻✻✻✻✻✻✻✻✻✻✻✻✻

EPILOGUE,

Written by D. GARRICK, Esq.

Spoken by Miss YOUNGE,

POST hafte from Italy arrives my Lover !
   Shall I to you, good Friends, my fears difcover ?
Should Foreign modes his Virtues mar, and mangle, .
And *Caro Spofo* prove—Sir *Dingle Dangle* ;
No fooner *join'd* than *feparate* we go,
Abroad—we never fhall each other know,
At home—I mope *above*—he'll pick his teeth *below.*   }
In fweet domeftic chat we ne'er fhall mingle,
And, *wedded* tho' I am, fhall ftill live *fingle,*
However modifh, I deteft this plan :
For me, no maukifh creature, weak, and wan;   }
He muft be *Englifh,* and an *Englifh*—Man.
To Nature, and his Country, falfe and blind,
Shou'd *Belville* dare to twift his form and mind,
I will difcard him—and to Britain true,
A Briton chufe—and, may be, one of *you !*
Nay; don't be frighten'd—I am but in jeft ;
Free Men in Love, or War, fhould ne'er be prefs'd,

   If you wou'd know my utmoft expeſtation,
'Tis one unfpoil'd by *travell'd* Education ;
With knowledge, tafte, much kindnefs, and fome whim,
Good fenfe to govern *me*—and let *me* govern him :
Great love of me, muft keep his heart from roving ;
Then. I'll forgive him, if he proves too loving :
If in thefe times, I fhou'd be blefs'd by Fate
With fuch a *Phœnix,* fuch a matchlefs Mate,
I will by kindnefs, and fome fmall difcerning,
Take care that *Hymen's* torch continues burning :
At weddings, now-a-days, the torch thrown down,
Juft makes a fmoke, then ftinks throughout the town !
No married Puritan—I'll follow pleafure,
And ev'n the Fafhion—but in mod'rate meafure ;

EPILOGUE,

I will of Op'ra extafies partake,
Tho' I take fnuff to keep myfelf awake;
No rampant Plumes fhall o'er my temples play,
Foretelling that my brains will fly away;
Nor from my head fhall ftrange vagaries fpring,
To fhew the foil can teem with ev'ry thing!
No *fruits, roots, greens*, fhall fill the ample fpace,
A *kitchen-garden*, to adorn my face!
No Rock. fhall there be feen, no Windmill, Fountain,
Nor curls like Guns fet round, to guard the Mountain!
O learn, ye Fair, if this fame madnefs fpreads,
Not to *hold up*, but to *keep down* your heads:
Be not mifled by ftrange fantaftic art,
But in your drefs let *Nature* take fome part;
Her fkill alone a lafting pow'r infures,
And beft can ornament fuch charms as *yours*.

PERSONS OF THE DRAMA.

M E N.

Mr. HARGRAVE	Mr. *Yates.*
GEORGE HARGRAVE	Mr. *Smith.*
Mr. DRUMMOND	Mr. *Benfley,*
Sir CHA. SEYMOUR	Mr. *Brereton.*
Mr. MORLEY	Mr. *Aickin.*
JUSTICE	Mr. *Parfons.*
JARVIS	Mr. *Palmer.*
Firft Hunter	Mr. *Bannifter.*

W O M E N.

Lady DINAH	Mrs. *Hopkins.*
BELLA	Mifs *Younge.*
EMILY	Mrs. *Siddons.*
HARRIET	Mifs *Hopkins.*
SUSAN	Mrs. *Wrighten.*

Gentlemen, Hunters, Servants, &c.

SCENE, Mr. *Hargrave*'s Houfe in the Country.

THE

RUNAWAY.

ACT I.

SCENE, *a Garden.*

BELLA *and* HARRIET. *Enter* GEORGE.

George.

OH, for the luxury of night-gown and flippers! No jaded hack of Parnaſſus can be more tired than I am—the roads ſo duſty, and the ſun ſo hot—'twould be leſs intolerable riding poſt in Africa.

Bella. What a wild imagination!—But in the name of Fortune, why are you alone? What have you done with all the College youths?—This is the firſt vacation you ever came home unaccompanied, and I aſſure you *we* are quite diſappointed.

Geo. Oh, moſt unconſcionable Woman! Never to be ſatisfied with conqueſt——There's poor Lumley ſhot through by your wicked eyes.

Bella. A notable victory indeed!——however, his name ſerves to make a figure in the liſts of one's conqueſts, and ſo you may give him juſt hope enough to feed his ſighs,—but not to encourage his preſumption.

Geo. Paragon of generoſity!——And what portion of comfort will your Ladyſhip beſtow on Egerton and Filmer, who ſtill hug the chains of the reſiſtleſs Arabella?

Bella. Upon my word, your catalogue grows intereſting—'tis worth while now to enquire for your vouchers——Proofs, George, proofs.

B

Geo. Why, the firſt writes ſonnets in your praiſe, and the laſt toaſts you till he can't ſee.

Bella. Oh, excellent !——The Dulcinea of one—and Circe of the other—ha! ha!—to transform him into a beaſt——I hope you have better love-tokens for the bluſhing Harriet——How does——

Harriet. Fye, Bella——you uſe me i

Geo. Why, Siſter, you plead guilty, ... the charge is exhibited——But tell me, my ſweet H . .   t, who is this favour'd mortal, of whom you mean to enquire?

Har. Indeed, Brother, I have no enquiries to make ; but I imagine my Couſin can inform you whom ſhe meant.

Bella. Oh, doubtleſs——but you look ſo offended, Harriet, that I dare not venture the enquiry : aſk for Sir Charles Seymour yourſelf.

Geo. Seymour ! Ho, ho ! Very fine truly ! [*aſide.*] If Seymour be the man, my Siſter, ſet your heart at reſt—— he is on the point of marriage, *if I am not miſtaken*, with a fine blooming Girl, not more than eighteen.——Soft, dove-like eyes—pouting lips—teeth that were, doubtleſs, made of oriental pearl—a neck—I want a ſimile now—— ivory, wax, alabaſter !—no; they won't do.

Har. [*with an air of pique.*] One would imagine, Brother, you were drawing the picture of your own Miſtreſs, inſtead of Sir Charles's, your colours are ſo warm.

Geo. A fine Woman, Harriet, gives warmth to all around her——She is that univerſal ſpirit, about which Philoſophers talk ; the true point of attraction that governs Nature, and controuls the univerſe of Man.

Bella. Heiday, George ! Did the charms of Lady Dinah inſpire this rhapſody ?

Geo. Charms ! What, of that antiquated, ſententious, delicate Lady, who bleſs'd us with her long ſpeeches at dinner ?

Bel. You muſt learn to be more reſpectful in your epithets, Sir ; for that ſententious, delicate Lady deſigns you the honour of becoming your Mother.

Geo. My Mother! Heaven forefend——you jeſt, ſurely.

Bel. You ſhall judge.——We met her in our late viſit to Bath—She renewed her acquaintance with your Father, with whom, in Mrs. Hargrave's life-time, ſhe had been intimate——He invited her to return with us, and ſhe has been here this month—They are frequently closeted together——She has *forty thousand pounds*, and is Sister to an Irish Peer.

Geo. She might have been Grandmother to the Peer, by the days she has numbered—But her excessive propriety and decorum overcome me——How can they agree with my father's vociferation, October, and hounds?

Bel. Oh, I assure you, wondrously well—she kisses Jowler, takes Ringwood on her lap, and has, more than once, sipp'd out of your Father's tankard.——Delicacies, Cousin, are easily made to give way, when we have certain ends to answer.

Geo. Very true; and beware of that period, when delicacies *must* give way—tremble at the hour, Bella, when you'll rise from the labours of your toilette with no end in view, but the conquest of some Quixote Galant in his grand climacteric——on whom you'll squander more encouraging glances, than all the sighs and ardor of two and twenty can extort from you now.

Bel. *Memento mori* ! Quite a College compliment: you ought rather to have supposed that my power will increase ; and that, like Ninon, I might give myself the airs of eighteen at eighty——But here's John coming to summon us to coffee.——Harriet !

Geo. Come, Harriet—why that pensive air ? Give me your hand.

Har. Excuse me—I'll only step and look at my birds, and follow you instantly——[*Exeunt* George *and* Bella *playfully.*]—" Set your heart at rest, my Sister." ——Oh, Brother !—you have robb'd that heart of rest for ever.—— Cruel intelligence !—Something has long sat heavy in my bosom—and now the weight is irremoveable —Perfidious Seymour !—yet, of what can I accuse him ? He never profess'd to love me—Oh yes, his ardent looks —his sighs—his confusion—his respectful attentions, have a thousand times profess'd the strongest passion.——Surely, a man cannot, in honour, be exculpated, who by such methods defrauds a Woman of her heart; even tho' the *word* Love should never pass his lips. Yet I ought not to have trusted these seeming proofs—no; I must only blame my own credulity——O partial Nature !—why have you given us hearts so replete with tenderness, and minds so weak, so yielding ?

SCENE, *a Garden Parlour.*

Enter GEORGE *and* BELLA *at the Garden Door.*

BELLA *seating herself at a Tea-table.*

Bel. Hang this Lady Dinah—one's forc'd to be so dress'd, and so formal!——In the country we should be all shepherds and shepherdesses—Meadows, ditches, rooks, and court-manners, are the strangest combination!

Geo. Hist—she's in the hall, I see—I'll go and 'squire her in. ·　[*Exit* George, *and returns with Lady* Dinah.

Lady D. To you, Sir, who have been so long conversant with the fine manners of the Antients, the frivolous custom of tea-drinking must appear ridiculous.

Geo. No custom can be ridiculous, Madam, that gives us the society of the Ladies—The young men of those days deserve your Ladyship's pity, for having never tasted these elegant hours.

Lady D. [*aside.*] He is just what his Father described.

Enter Mr. HARGRAVE.

Mr. H. No;—Barbary Bess is spavin'd; let her be taken care of: I'll have Longshanks, and see that he's saddled by five——So we sha'n't have you in the hunt to-morrow, George,—you must have more time to shake off the lazy rust of Cambridge, I suppose.——What sort of hours d'ye keep at College?

Geo. Oh, Sir, we are frequently up before the Sun, there.

Mr. H. Hah!—then 'tis when you ha'n't been in bed all night, I believe.——And how do you stand in other matters?—Have the musty old Dons tired you with their Greek, and their Geometry, and their learned Experiments to shew what air, and fire, and water, are made of? Ha! ha! ha!

Bella. Oh, no, Sir—he never studied them closely enough to be tired—his Philosophy and mine keep pretty equal pace, I believe.

Geo. As usual, my lively Cousin ——If you had said my Philosophy and your Coquetry, I should have thought you had meant to compliment me—However, Sir, I am not tired of my studies—though Bella has not exactly hit the reason.

Lady D. to *Mr. H.* The Mufes, Sir, fufficiently recompence the moſt painful affiduities by which we obtain their favour—Their *true* lovers are never fatiated with the pleaſures they beſtow—thoſe, indeed, who court them, like the Toaſts of the ſeaſon, *becauſe* it is the faſhion, are neither warm'd by their beauties, nor penetrated with their charms—but theſe are faithleſs Knights ;—your Son, I dare ſay, has enliſted himſelf among their ſincereſt Votaries.

Geo. You do me great honour, Madam,—I have no doubt but you are perfectly acquainted with the Mufes. They ſhed their favours on a few only—but thoſe who ſhare them muſt, like you, be irreſiſtible. I'll catch her Ladyſhip's ſtyle.   [*aſide.*

Mr. H. [*aſide.*] Humph—I am glad he likes her.

Lady Dinah. You men are ſo full of flattery ! In Athens, in Lacedemon, that vice was for ages unknown—it was then the Athenians were the happieſt, and the Lacedemonians the—

Bella. Oh mercy !—I have burnt my fingers in the moſt terrible manner.   [*Enter* Harriet *from the Garden.*] I wiſh the misfortune had happened to her Ladyſhip's tongue.   [*aſide.*

Har. Dear Bella, I am quite concerned.

Bella. Pho !—I only meant to break in upon her harangue, there's no bearing ſo much Wiſdom.

                               [*Enter* Servant.

Serv. Mr. Drummond.

Enter *Mr.* DRUMMOND,

Mr. D. Benedicite !—ah !—my dear Godſon !—— why, this is an unexpected pleaſure—I did not know you were arrived.

Geo. I have had that happineſs only a few hours, Sir, and I was on the point of paying my devoirs to you at the Park.

Mr. D. Ungracious Rogue ! a few hours, and not been with me yet !—however—ſtay where you are, ſtay where you are, George—you cannot come under my roof with ſafety now, I aſſure you ; ſuch a pair of eyes, ſuch a bloom, ſuch a ſhape !——Ah Girls, Girls !

Har. Dear Mr. Drummond, of what, or whom, are you talking ? You make me quite jealous,

Mr. D. Oh! you are all out-done, eclipfed—you have no chance with my *Incognita*—Then fhe has the prettieft foot—and moves a Grace !

Bel. Teafing creature !

Mr. D. Pretty Bella!—well, it fhall be fatisfied. Mr. Hargrave, I wait on you, Sir, to requeft an apartment for a young Lady of beauty, and honour, who hath put herfelf under my protection.—But as I really think my houfe a dangerous fituation for her, confidering that I am fingle, young and handfome, [*ftroking his face*] I cannot in confcience expofe her to it.—You, being a grave, orderly man, and having a couple of decent, well-behaved young women for a Daughter and Niece; I think fhe will be more agreeably protected here—and this is my bufinefs.

Mr. H. A young Lady who hath put herfelf under your protection ! Who is fhe ?

Mr. D. Her name fhe wifhes to conceal.

Mr. H. That's very odd—Where did you meet with her ?

Mr. D. At the houfe of a Widow Tenant of mine, a few miles from hence, where fhe had taken refuge from a marriage to which an Uncle would have forced her.—She had no companion but the good old Lady, whom I found employed in affifting her to weep, inftead of confoling her.—In fhort, there were *reafons* to think her fituation highly dangerous, and I prevail'd on her to leave it.

Har. And fo your credulity is again taken in, and the air of a weeping Beauty is the trap that caught you? —Ha, ha! ha!—Will you never be fick of impofitions ?

Mr. D. I don't remember that I was ever impofed on.

Mr. H. No! don't I know how many people you have plagued yourfelf about, who had not a grain of merit to deferve it ?

Mr. D. I want *merit* Mr. Hargrave; yet all the bleffings of health and fortune have not been with-held from *me*.

Mr. H. Aye, aye—there's no getting you to hear reafon on this fubject.

Mr. D. 'Tis too late to reafon now. The young Lady is at my houfe—I have promifed to bring her here, and we muft endeavour to raife the poor Girl's fpirits. She would have fpoil'd the prettieft face in England— beg pardon, Ladies—*one* of the prettieft faces, with weeping at the old Widows.

Bel. An old Widow, a pretty Girl, a Lover, a tyran-
nical Uncle—'tis a charming group for the amufement of
a village circle.—I long to fee this Beauty.

Lady D. Her beauty, according to Mr. Drummond,
may be confpicuous enough—but her pretenfions to *birth*
and *honour* feem to be a more doubtful matter.

Geo. Pardon me, Madam, why fhould we doubt of
either? A Lady in fuch a fituation has a right to protection; [*to his Father*] and I hope, Sir, you will not with-
hold yours.

Mr. H. Oh, no, to be fure, George.—'Sbud! refufe
protection to a fine Girl!—'twould be, with you, a crying
Sin, I warrant—but Mr. Drummond, I fhould fuppofe—

Mr. D. Come, be fatisfied, the weakneffes with
which you reproach me, might have induced me to have
fnatched her from an alarming fituation without much
examination.—But, in compliment to your delicacy, I
have made proper enquiries.—She was placed under the
care of Mrs. Carlton by a perfon of credit.—She has dif-
patched a meffenger to her Uncle, who, I prefume, will
be here to-morrow.

Har. Pray, Sir, permit us to wait on the Lady,
and conduct her here; I am ftrongly interefted for her.

Mr. H. 'Tis an odd affair——what fay you to it, my
Lady?

Lady D. As your Family feem defirous to receive her,
Sir, I am forry to perceive an impropriety in the requeft—
but I fhould apprehend that any appearance of encouragement to young Ladies in *difobedience*—particularly when
accompanied with the glaring indecorum of an elope-
ment—

Mr. H. Aye, very true——'Sbud, Mr. Drummond,
how can you encourage fuch—

Mr. D. Madam, I do not mean to encourage, but
to reftore the young Lady to her family. She feems
terrified at the peculiar feverity of her Uncle's temper; fo
we'll put ourfelves in form, receive him in full affembly,
and divide his anger amongft us.—Your Ladyfhip, I'm
fure, muft be happy to render the recovery of the *firft falfe
ftep* as eafy as poffible.

Mr. H. Why aye, my Lady—there can be no harm
in that, you know.

Lady D. Very well, Sir—if you think fo, I can have
no farther objection.

Mr. H. Well then, Harriet, you may go—I think.

Bella. And I with you, Cousin.

Mr. D. Come then, my pretty doves——I'll escort you.——George, steel your heart, steel your heart, you Rogue.   [*Exeunt.*

Geo. It is steel'd, Sir.

Mr. H. You need not go, George—I want to speak to you.

Lady D. Bless me!—what does he intend to say now?— he's going to open the affair to his Son—well—these are the most aukward moments in a Woman's life—but one must go through it. [*aside.*] I have letters to write, which I'll take this leisure to do, if you'll pardon my absence, Gentlemen.

Mr. H. To be sure, Madam [*both bowing. Exit Lady D.*]—Well, George, how do you like that Lady?

Geo. *Extravagantly,* Sir,——I never saw a Lady so learn'd.

Mr. H. Oh, she's clever—she's an Earl's Sister too, and a forty thousand pounder, boy.

Geo. That's a fine fortune.

Mr. H. Aye, very fine, very fine—and then her interest!—suppose I could prevail with her—eh, George—if one could keep her in the family, I say—would not that be a stroke?

Geo. An alliance with so noble a family, Sir, is certainly a desirable circumstance.

Enter Servant.

Ser. The Gentlemen are in the smoaking parlour, Sir.

Mr. H. Very well—are the pipes and October in readiness?

Ser. Yes, Sir.   [*Exit.*

Mr. H. Well then, we'll talk over the affair to-morrow—what—I suppose your stomach is too squeamish for tobacco and strong beer?——you'll find the Justice, and some more of your old friends there.

Geo. Pardon me, Sir, I made too free with the bottle at dinner, and have felt the effects in my head ever since —I believe a turn in the garden is a better recipe than the fumes of tobacco.

Mr. H. Well, well, we won't dispute the matter with you now, boy—but you know I don't like milksops.

Geo. [*smiling.*] Nor I, Sir.   [*Bows and exit.*

Mr. H. Aye, aye, George is a brave Boy—Old England is disgraced by a set of whipsters who affect to despise the jolly manners of their Ancestors, while they only serve to shew us, how greatly manners may be *alter'd* without being *mended*—

Enter JUSTICE.

'Sbud, I don't know that we are a bit wiser, happier, or greater, than we were in good old Bess's days—when our Men of Rank were robust, and our Women of Fashion buxom.

Justice. Aye, aye, a plague on all the innovations that tend to produce a race of *pretty fellows* instead of *Englishmen*—and puny girls, for the Mothers of Heroes—Give me a rosy buxom lass, with eyes that sparkle like the glasses we toast her in——adad, I'd drink her health till the world danced round like a top—But, what a plague, 'Squire, d'ye stay here for? come into t'other room, and if you have a mind to make wise speeches there, we can drink in the mean time, and then what you say will have a proper effect.

Mr. H. Well, well, I'll go, but I want to consult you——I have been thinking whether this Greenwood estate—

Jus. Tush—you know very well, I can neither consider or advise, till I have had my brace—I am as dark, till the liquor sends its spirits into my brains, as a lantern without its candle—so, if you've any knotty point to propose, keep it till I'm enlighten'd.

Mr. H. Well, come along. *{Going. Enter Clerk.}*

Cl. The people from the Crown, Sir, and the Rose, and the Antelope, are here again about their licences.

Jus. [*To Mr. H.*] There——this is what I got by coming for you—I charged the Butler not to let t this dog in.—[*to the clerk*] Why, how can I help it?—bid 'em come again to-morrow—'tis of no consequence.

Cl. And here's a Pauper to be pass'd——a lame Man with four Children.

Har. Well, turn him over to the Cook, and let him wait till we are at leisure.

Cl. And a Constable has brought up a man, for breaking into farmer Thompson's barn last night.

Jus. Has he? [*seeming irresolute*] well, tell him to wait too—we are going to be busy now, and can't be disturb'd. But bid him take care he doesn't let the prisoner escape, as he did that dog Farlow, d'ye hear?

C

Cl. Yes, Sir—-but—-Juſtice Manly is now in the ſmoaking-room—I've ſpoke to him about the licences, and we may'nt have another bench this——

Juſ. Will you pleaſe to march, Sir ?　[*Exit Clerk.*

Mr. H. Well done, old Boy—-Burn himſelf could not have diſpatch'd buſineſs with more expedition.
　　　　　　　　　　　　　　[*Going. Enter Servant.*

Ser. The Miller is here, Sir, with a man that he cotch'd with a hare that he had taken in the ſpringe— but the poor fellow, pleaſe your Honour, has a large family.　　　　　　　　　　[Hargr. *and the Juſtice return.*

Mr. H. What ! a Hare—Come along, Juſtice.
　　　　　　　　　　　　　　　　　[*Exit another way.*

A burſt of laughter from the ſmoaking room.——the Juſtice looks wiſtfully back, and then follows Mr. Hargrave.

S C E N E, *the Garden.*
Enter GEORGE *reading.*

Geo. Here's a ſpecial Fellow of a Philoſopher now— would perſuade that Pleaſure has no exiſtence, when bounteous Nature teems with her——ſhe courts my ſenſes in a thouſand varied modes— She poſſeſſes herſelf of my underſtanding in the ſhape of Reaſon—and ſhe ſeizes my heart in the form of Woman, dear, beauteous, all-ſubduing Woman. And there is one—Memory, be faithful to her charms ! Shew me the beauteous form, the animated face, the mind that beam'd in her eyes—the bluſhing ſmile that repaid my admiration, and raiſed an altar in my heart, on which every other paſſion is ſacrificed—on which every hope, deſire, and wiſh, is ſanctified by her.

Enter BELLA.

Bella. Oh, monſtrous—George Hargrave moralizing in the garden, whilſt the fineſt girl in England is in the parlour !—what is become of your gallantry ?

Geo. Gone, ſweet Couſin, gone.

Bel. Indeed ! who has robb'd you of it ?

Geo. A Woman.

Bel. Come then, and regain it from a Woman, and ſuch a Woman—

Geo. Is ſhe ſo beautiful ?

Bel. Beautiful ! look at me,—I myſelf am not ſo handſome.

Geo. Ha ! ha ! ha !—that, I confeſs, is an infallible criterion.—But I'll bet this whole volume of Wiſdom, againſt one of your Billet-doux, that ſhe's not within fifty degrees of her who witch'd away my heart.

Bel. Witch'd it indeed, if in ſix weeks it has not made one excurſion—I never knew you ſo conſtant before. However, I prophesy *her* charm is broke ; the Divinity who will reign—perhaps for another ſix weeks—is coming down the ſteps with Harriet—but, that her rays may not dazzle your mortal ſight, ſhelter yourſelf behind the clump, and examine her. [*George goes and returns.* Well, how d'ye like her ?

Geo. Like her !—the air is all Ambroſia—every happy conſtellation is in conjunction—each bounteous ſtar has lent its influence, and Venus guided the event.

Bel. Heyday—what event ? Sure this cannot be your Maſquerade Lady !

Geo. It is, it is—ſhe is the ſweet Thief—ſhe is my Wood Nymph—Oh, I am tranſported !

Bel. And I—amazed !—how can it—

Geo. No matter how—whether by chance or witchcraft—Now could I apoſtrophize—Pſhaw—away, and at her feet—theſe tranſports— [*Going.*

Enter Mr. DRUMMOND.

Mr. Drum. So, ſo, ſo,—and pray, what's the cauſe of theſe tranſports ?

Geo. You are the cauſe—'tis to you, my dear Mr. Drummond, I am indebted for the happineſs which dawns on me.

Mr. Drum. Then, God grant, my dear Boy, the dawn may not deceive thee—I wiſh it to brighten into the faireſt day—But how have I been inſtrumental to all this ?

Geo. That Lady I have ſeen before at a Maſquerade —She poſſeſſed herſelf of my heart at once, but I deſpair'd of ever beholding her again—Pray preſent me— [*Going.*]

Mr. Drum. Hold, George, hold—perhaps you'd better never be preſented ; for, tho' you may have put her in poſſeſſion of your heart, 'tis by no means an evidence, that ſhe has had the ſame complaiſance for you—Suppoſe, for inſtance, ſuch a trifle as *hers* being engaged.

Bella. Oh unconſcionable ! to fancy the galloping imagination of a man in love, capable of ſo *reaſonable* a ſuppoſition !—But, pray have ſo much decency, George, to poſtpone your *entrée* till you are more compoſed, I'll go, and prepare her for the reception of a ſtrange creature, that you may appear to advantage.   [Exit.

Geo. · Advantage ! oh, I will hope every advantage, from ſo fortunate a chance—her heart cannot—ſhall not be engaged—and ſhe ſhall be mine—Pardon, my dear Sir, theſe effuſions of my joy.

Mr. D. I do pardon them—'tis an odd circumſtance, —Are you acquainted with the Lady's name ?

Geo. No one knew her—She ſeemed like an Angel deſcended to aſtoniſh her beholders, and vaniſh the moment ſhe had fixt their hearts—Unluckily Mrs. Fitzherbert ſtopt me, and a jealous coxcomb in her train ſeized that moment, to hurry her out of the room.

Mr. D. That misfortune, perhaps, I can repair— but you ſeem ſo extravagantly diſpoſed to raptures, that I hardly dare tell you I know ſomething of her family.

Geo. I am rejoiced—for I am convinced you know nothing that will not juſtify my paſſion.

Mr. D. This eagerneſs to *believe* might have been ſo fatal, that I tremble for you—But you are fortunate—ſhe is the Daughter of a deceaſed Major Morley—a man, to whoſe friendſhip, and elegance of manners, I was indebted for happy and rational hours, amidſt the buſtle of a Camp.

Geo. Fortunate indeed ! for then my paſſion muſt have *your* ſanction—but I thought you had not known—

Mr. D. I knew her Father's picture on her arm—but her delicacy is ſo alarmed at the idea of expoſing the name of her Family in ſuch a ſituation, that ſhe would not conſent to be introduced here, but on condition of its being conceal'd.

Geo. Charming delicacy ! I will keep her ſecret. My only conſolation was, that ſuch a Woman could not be long concealed, and it would have been the buſineſs of my life, till I had diſcover'd her— · but your goodneſs has brought about the event—your goodneſs, to which I owe more than——

Mr. D. · Nay, ſtop your acknowledgements, and don't arrogate to your own merits the affection I have for you ; for, tranſcendent as without doubt they are, you owe great part of it to circumſtances, in which they have very little concern.

· *Geo.* · I am contented to hold your eſteem by any tie——But, dear Sir, the Lady——

Mr. D. Impatient Rogue !—Well, come, I'll introduce you, and may the moment be auſpicious !   [Exit.

Geo. May it! Oh Love, sweet Tyrant! I yield my heart to thee a willing slave—to Love I devote my future life—never more shall I experience the aching void of indifference, or know one moment unoccupied by thee.

[*Exit.*

END OF THE FIRST ACT.

✿✿✿✿✿✿✿✿✿✿✿✿✿✿✿✿✿✿✿✿✿✿✿

ACT II.

SCENE, *a Court before the House.*

Enter a HUNT. *A Flourish of Horns.*

Hollo! hollo! ye hoicks, Hargrave, ille, ille, hoa.

First Hunter.

ZOUNDS, 'tis almost seven;—[*looking at his watch*] the scent will be cold—let's rouse the lazy rogue with a song.

Second Hunt. Aye, a good thought—come, begin.

SONG.

Arouse, and break the bands of sleep;
Blush, Idler, blush, such hours to keep.
Somnus! what bliss canst thou bestow,
Equal to that which Hunters know,
Whether the mountains they attain,
Or swiftly dart across the plain?
Somnus! what joys canst thou bestow,
Equal to those which Hunters know?
Hark thro' the wood, how our music resounds!
The horns re-ecchoed, more sweet by the hounds.
Deep-throated and clear,
Our spirits they cheer;
They give us such glee,
No danger we see,
But follow with pleasure:
'Tis joy beyond measure
To be the first in at the death—at the death,
To be, &c.

Enter GEORGE *from the House.*

First Gent. Hah, my young Hercules!——But how now, in this dress! don't you hunt with us?

Geo. Oh, I have only changed liveries,—I ufed to wear
that of Adonis—but now I ferve his miftrefs—Venus.

Second Gent. And a moft hazardous fervice you have
chofen—I would rather fubject myfelf to the fate of Acteon, than to the caprice and infolence of the handfomeft
Coquette in England.

Geo. Acteon's fate would be lefs than you'd deferve,
if, knowing my Goddefs, you fhould dare profane her
with fuch epithets.

Second Gent. May I never ftart Pufs, if I believe your
Goddefs to be more than a very Woman——that is, a
being whofe foul is vanity—tafte, voluptuoufnefs—form,
deceitful—and manners, unnatural.

Geo. Heyday!—turn'd Satyrift on the fex at eight
and twenty!——What jilting Blowfalind has work'd
this miracle ?

Second Gent. Faith, I take my copies from higher
fchools——Amongft the Blowfalinds there is ftill Nature
and Honefty—but examine our Drawing-rooms, Ope-
ras, and Water-drinking places—you'll find the firft
turn'd fairly out of doors, and the laft exchanged for Affectation and Hypocrify—fo henceforward [*fmacking his
whip*] I abandon all Ladies, but thofe of the woods,
and chafe only the harmlefs game, to which my fagacious
hounds conduct me.   [*Exit.*

Geo. Ha! ha!—and in a fhort time be fit fociety for
your hounds only. Good morning, Sir.

Enter Mr. HARGRAVE *and the* Juftice.

Mr. H. So, George—Come, you'd better mount—
I'll give you a Lecture upon Air, and the advantages of a
good Conftitution, on our Downs, worth all you cou'd
hear in a mufty College thefe fifty years.

Geo. I beg, Sir, to be excus'd this morning——to-
morrow I'll refume my ufual poft, and lead where you
only will venture to follow me.

Mr. H. Well—we fhall put you to the teft. [*Exit.*

Juftice to Geo. Yes, yes, you're a keen Sportfman—
I faw the Game you are in purfuit of, fcudding away to
the garden—beat the bufhes, and I'll warrant you'll ftart
her, and run her down too.

Third Gent. Egad! I ftarted a fine young Pufs a few
days ago——She feem'd fhy, and made her doublings;
but I ftuck to the fcent, and fhou'd infallibly have got
her, if that fly poaching rogue, Drummond, had not laid
a fpringe in her way.

Juſtice. Why, ſhe's the very Puſs I mean; he hous'd her here. [*Exit.*

· *Third Gent.* Oh, ho! then I ſuppoſe he only pointed
· the game for you——Sweet Sir, your humble——After
· College commons, a coarſer diſh than Pheaſant, I think,
· might have gone down.

Geo. · Your whip, Sir—your bit wants laſhing. To
· talk thus of Mr. Drummond, whom you *do* know, is
· not more infolent than your profanation of a Lady
· whom you do *not* know.

Third Gent. · O! cry you mercy—Plague take me if I
· quarrel for any wench in England—You are heartily
· welcome to her, Sir, only I hope another time you'll be
· honeſt, and hunt without a ſtalking-horſe. [*Exit.*

Geo. Barbarian! How critically did Mr. Drummond
relieve the lovely Girl——This brute had diſcovered her,
and ſhe would have ſuffered every indignity that Ignorance, ſupported by the pride of Fortune, could have in-
flicted. In the garden—that's fortunate beyond my ex-
pectations—'midſt groves and fountains—the very ſcene
where a lover ſhould tell his tale---and the ſweet conſci-
ouſneſs which beamed in her eyes laſt night, flatters me
that ſhe will not *hate* me for my tale——I'll go in all the
confidence of hope. [*Exit.*

SCENE, *the Garden.*

Enter EMILY.

Em. What an heavenly morning!—ſurely'tis in England that Summer keeps her court—for ſhe's no where
elſe ſo lovely.—And what a ſweet garden this is!—But
tell me, my heart—is it the brightneſs of the morning, the
verdure of the garden, the melody of the birds, that gives
thee theſe enchanting ſenſations?—Ah, no!—it is that
thou haſt found thy Lord—it is, that I have again ſeen
the Man, who, ſince I firſt beheld him, has been the only
image in my mind.—How different from the empty, the
preſuming Baldwin!—yet, I owe *him* this obligation—if
his hateful perſeverance had not forced me from London,
I might never have ſeen, but once, the Man who, *that
once*, poſſeſs'd himſelf of my tendereſt wiſhes.— Ha!
[*ſtarting.*] *Enter* GEORGE.

Geo. Abroad ſo early, Madam!—the fine Ladies in
London are yet in their firſt ſleep.

Em. It would have been impoffible to have refifted the chearful call of the Hunters, if the morning had been lefs enticing.

Geo. Oh, do not imagine yourfelf obliged to the Hunters, Madam, it was my good Genius—I thank her—that infpired them, and did me the favour to lead me here.

Em. If fhe ufually influences you to no better purpofe, her claims to your gratitude are but weak.

Geo. 'Till lately I thought fo, and fuppofed myfelf influenced by the worft Genius that ever fell to the lot of a poor mortal—but fhe has entirely retrieved herfelf in my opinion, and by two or three capital ftrokes has made me forget her unlucky pranks, and believe her one of the beft difpofed Sylphs in all the regions of Fancy.

Em. [*fmiling.*] You recommend this aërial attendant very ftrongly—Have you any intention to part from her?

Geo. I would willingly exchange her—if your Genius would be fo obliging to take a fancy to me—I'll accept her with all my heart—and give you mine.

Em. You wou'd lofe by the exchange.

Geo. Impoffible!—for my quondam friend would fay a thoufand things for me, that I could not for myfelf—fo I fhould gain your good opinion—and that would be *well gained*, whatever I might lofe to attain it.

Em. Your Genius is, at leaft, a gallant one, I perceive—but I was on the point of leaving the garden, Sir.——The Ladies, I imagine, are rifen by this time.

Geo. Indeed they are not, but if they fhould—thefe are precious moments, which I muft not lofe—may I prefume to ufe them in telling you how happy I am, in the event which placed you in my Father's houfe?—but you have, perhaps, forgot the prefumptuous Tancred, who gave fuch difturbance to the Gentleman honour'd by protecting you, at the Mafquerade?

Em. No, Sir, I remember—and, if I don't miftake, you were nearly engaged in a *fracas* with that Gentleman—I was happy, when I obferv'd you ftopt by a mafk, and feized that moment to leave the room.

Geo. A moment, Madam, that I have never ceas'd to regret 'till now—but *that* which I at prefent poffefs, is a felicity fo unexpected, and unhop'd for—

Em. You forget, Sir, thefe gallantries are out of place here—under a mafk, a Shepherd may figh, or an Eaftern Prince amufe himfelf in faying the moft extravagant things—but they know there are delicacies to be obferved in real life, quite incompatible with the freedoms of a Mafquerade.

Geo. 'Whilft you are thus fevere on mere gallantries, I will venture to hope that a moft tender and refpectful paffion will be treated more favourably.

Em. Sir!

Geo. · I comprehend, Madam, what your delicacy muft feel, and will therefore only add, that from the firft moment I beheld you, my heart has known no other object. *You* have been the Miftrefs of its Wifhes—and you *are* the Miftrefs of its Fate.

Em. (*hefitatingly*) Indeed, Sir, this declaration, at a time when I muft appear in fo ftrange a light to your family, hurts me greatly—I can fcarcely believe you mean it a compliment—but, furely, my fituation here ought—

Geo. I acknowledge, Madam, the confeffion I have dared to make, is premature—it is ill timed—nothing can excufe it, but the peculiarity of our fituation.——When I reflect, that in a few moments your Uncle may arrive, that he may fnatch you from us, and that fuch an opportunity never may be mine again—— [*Enter Mr.* Drummond.

Mr. D. So, fo, my young ones, have I found you? 'tis a moft delicious morning—but is it ufual with you, Madam, to tafte the air fo early?

Em. Yes, Sir—in the Country, at leaft—I feldom murder fuch hours in fleep.

Mr. D. Aye, 'tis to that practice you are indebted for the rofes in your cheeks—What, I fuppofe, you brought the Lady into the garden, George, to read her a lecture on Vegetation——to explain the nature and caufe of Heat——or, perhaps, more abftracted fubjects have engaged——

Geo. Stop, dear Sir—I affure you I am not abftracted enough to enter on thefe fubjects with fuch an object before me—I found the Lady here, and had fcarcely paid her my morning compliments when you appeared.

Mr. D. · For which you do not thank me, I prefume.—— but come, Madam, you are *my* ward, 'till I have the pleafure of prefenting you to your Uncle; and I come to conduct you to breakfaft. George, you may follow; but take care you keep your diftance. [*Exeunt Mr. D. and* Emily.

Geo. Diftance!—as well might you perfuade the fhadow to forfake its Sun, or erring mortals give up hopes of mercy.

D

——With what sweet confidence she gives her hand to Mr Drummond !——if these are the privileges of Age, I'll be young no longer.   [*Exit.*

SCENE, *Lady* DINAH's *Dressing-Room.*

Lady Dinah *dressing,* Susan *attending.*

Lady Dinah. Both in the garden— and in deep conversation!

Susan. It appear'd so, my Lady, as I saw them from the window—he looked eagerly in her face; and she blush'd, and seem'd confused.

Lady D. Confused indeed !——yes, so the Impertinent affected to appear last night—tho' it was evident she had neither eyes nor thoughts but for Mr. Hargrave's Son—who paid her those attentions which, from the present habits of life, are paid to *every* Woman—tho', I think, Mr. George Hargrave should be superior to these modern gallantries.

Suf. I dares to say she is some impostor——Husbands in good truth are not so plenty, that a woman need run away to escape one.

Lady D. I have no doubt of her being a low person—and as to her prettiness, 'tis of the kind one sees in wooden Dolls —cherry-colour cheeks, and eyes, that from the total absence of expression might be taken for glass.

Suf. I wonder Mr. Hargrave did not stand by his own opinion, and let her stay where she was; but whatever Mr. Drummond says is law here.

Lady D. Because Mr. Hargrave imagines he'll make his Son his heir—but if he does, he'll only share with the paupers of the neighbouring villages; for these Mr. Drummond seems to consider his family; and I am mistaken, if he does n't find it a pretty expensive one.

Suf. Oh, Ma'am, he believes every melancholy tale that's told him as a proof of his piety—Here's the Bow, my Lady— but as he fancies her prettyness was in danger, he had better have kept her in his own house, and stood guard himself.

Lady D. Aye—that employment, or any other that would keep him at home, might be useful—Want of rest [*looking in the glass*] absolutely transforms me—the detestable Horns, and their noisy accompanyment, waked me from the most delightful dream—How do I look to-day, Susan?

Suf. Oh, charmingly, my Lady.

Lady D. 'Tis a moſt provoking circumſtance, the colour of my hair ſhould be ſo ſoon changed—but Mrs. Gibſon's Liquid entirely hides that accident, I believe.

Suſ. Entirely, my Lady—and then, her Bloom, it is im-poſſible to diſtinguiſh from nature.

Lady D. You need not ſpeak ſo loud. In compliance with the cuſtom of modern times, a woman is forced to keep the uſe of theſe ſort of things as ſecretly as ſhe would an Illegitimate Birth. It was not ſo among the Antients——The Roman Ladies made a point of excelling in Arts of this kind; and the Empreſs Poppea was not aſhamed to carry in her train five hundred Aſſes, in whoſe milk ſhe bathed every morning for the benefit of her complexion.

Suſ. Five hundred Aſſes in one Lady's train!——thank Heaven, we have no ſuch engroſſing now-a-days—*our* Toaſts have all their full ſhare.

Lady D. Indeed! Mrs. Suſan, [*half ſmiling*] this wench has ideas. Pray, what do you think of the young Collegian?

Suſ. Oh, my Lady, he is the ſweeteſt, ſmarteſt Man—I think he is exactly like the picture of your Ladyſhip's Brother, that died when he was eighteen.

Lady D. People uſed to ſay *that* Brother, and myſelf, bore a ſtrong reſemblance.

Suſ. I dare to ſay you did, my Lady; for there's ſomething in the turn of young Mr. Hargrave's face, vaſtly like your Ladyſhip's. [*laughing behind her.*]

Lady D. Well, Suſan—I believe I may truſt you—I think you can be faithful.

Suſ. Moſt ſurely, my Lady—I would rather die than be-tray your Ladyſhip.

Lady D. Well, then—I proteſt I hardly know how to acknowledge it—But—

Suſan. But what, my Lady?——your Ladyſhip alarms me.

Lady D. I too am alarm'd—but I know your faith——[*ſighs.*] There will ſoon be a moſt intimate and never to be diſſolved connexion between me—and—young Mr. Hargrave.

Suſ. Young Mr. Hargrave, Madam!

Lady D. Yes, Young Mr. Hargrave, Madam——What doſt ſtretch thy eyes ſo widely at, wench?——Mr. George Hargrave, I ſay, is to be my Huſband——I am to be his Wife——Is it paſt thy comprehenſion?

Suf. I moſt humbly beg your Ladyſhip's pardon——it was my ſurpriſe—the whole houſe concludes your Ladyſhip is to marry Old Mr. Hargrave—but, to be ſure, the Son is a much more ſuitable match for your Ladyſhip.

Lady D. Old Mr. Hargrave, indeed !——the whole houſe. is very impertinent in its concluſions——Go, and bring the Bergamot hither. [*Exit* Suſ.] I marry Old Mr. Hargrave ! monſtrous abſurdity ! and by ſo prepoſterous an union to become the mother of that fine fellow, his Son !—'twould be inſupportable——no, Miſtreſs Suſan, 'tis Young Mr. Hargrave I am to marry. [*Enter* Suſan *with the Bergamot.*]— Here, ſcent that handkerchief, while I write to my agent to prepare matters for the writings. [*Exit.* Suſan *alone, ſcenting the handkerchief.*

Suf. To prepare matters for the writings ! a very fine buſineſs indeed ; and what you'll ſorely repent of, my good Lady, take my word for it——All thoſe ſcented waters, nor any other waters, will be able to keep up your ſpirits this time twelvemonth——A " *never to be diſſolved connexion,*" between fifty and twenty-one, ha ! ha ! ha !—I ſhall burſt with the ridiculous ſecret—I muſt find Jarvis, and give it vent——" never to be diſſolved connexion !"—ha, ha, ha !

[*Exit,*

S C E N E, an *Apartment.*

Enter GEORGE, HARRIET, *and* BELLA.

Bel. What transformations this Love can make ! You look as grave, George, and ſpeak as ſententiouſly, as an Old-Bailey Fortune-teller.

Geo. And is it only to preſerve your ſpirits, Bella, that you keep your heart ſo cold ?

Bel. The recipe is certainly not a bad one, if we may judge from the effects of the oppoſite element on *your* ſpirits —but I adviſe you, whatever you do, not to aſſume an appearance of gravity—'tis the moſt dangerous character in the world.

Geo. How ſo ?

Bel. Oh, the advantages you would loſe by it are inconconceivable. While you can ſuſtain that of a giddy, thoughtleſs, undeſigning, *great Boy,* all the impertinent and fooliſh things you commit will be excuſ'd—laugh'd at—nay, if accompanied by a certain manner, they will be applauded ——but do the ſame things with a grave reflecting face, and an important air—and you'll be condemn'd, *nem. con.*

Enter Servant.

Serv. Sir Charles Seymour is driving up the avenue, Sir.
[*Exit.*

Geo. Is he ?——I am rejoiced——

Har. Sir Charles Seymour, Brother ?——I thought you told us yefterday he was on the point of marriage.

Geo. Well, my dear Harriet, and what then ? Is his being on the point of marriage any reafon why he fhould not be here ?——he is even now haftening to pay his devoirs to the Lady——I left him yefterday at a friend's houfe on the road, and he promifed to call on us in his way to-day—— but I hear him— [*Exit.*

Bel. Harriet, you look quite pale——I had no concep-tion that Sir Charles was of *ferious* confequence to you.

Har. My dear Bella—I am afhamed of myfelf—I'll go with you to your dreffing-room—I muft not fee him while I look fo ridiculoufly——I dread my Brother's raillery.

Bel. Come then, hold by me.. Deuce take it, what bu-finefs have women with hearts ?—If I could influence the Houfe, handfome men fhould be fhut out of fociety, 'till they grew harmlefs, by becoming Hufbands. [*Exeunt.*

Enter GEORGE *and* Sir CHARLES.

Geo. Ha ! the birds are flown.

Sir Cha. Let us purfue 'em then.

Geo. Pho—they are not worth purfuing——Bella's a Co-quette, and Harriet's in love.

Sir Ch. Harriet in love !

Geo. Aye, fhe's in for't, depend on't—but that's nothing, I have intelligence for the man—my *Incognita's* found, fhe's now in the houfe—my beauteous Wood Nymph !

Sir Ch. Mifs Hargrave's heart another's !

Geo. Mifs Hargrave's heart another's—why, my Sifter's heart is certainly engaged—but how's all this ?

Sir Ch. O George ! I love—I love your Sifter—to diftrac-tion, doat on her.

Geo. A pretty time, for the mountain to give up its bur-then truly ! Why did you not tell me this before ? If your heart had been as open to me, as mine has ever been to you— I might have ferv'd you ; but now—

Sir Ch. Oh, reproach me not, but pity me—I love your Sifter—long have lov'd her.

Geo. And not intruft your love *to me !*—You diftrufted me, Charles, and you'll be *properly* punifh'd.

Sir Ch. Severely am I punifh'd—fool, fool, that I was, thus to have built a fuperftructure of happinefs for all my life to come, that in one moment diffolves into air ! I cannot fee your Sifter—I muft leave you.

Geo. Indeed, you fhall not leave me, Seymour—On what grounds did you build your hopes, that you feem fo greatly difappointed ?—Had my Sifter accepted your addreffes ?

Sir Ch. No—I never prefumed to make her any—my fortune was fo fmall, that I had no hopes of obtaining your Father's confent—and therefore made it a point of honour not to endeavour to gain her affection.

Geo. Yes, yes, you took great care. . .   [*afide.*

Sir Ch. But my Uncle's death having removed every caufe of fear on that head, I flatter'd myfelf I had nothing elfe to apprehend.

Geo. Courage, my friend, and your difficulties may vanifh. 'Tis your humble diftant lovers who have fung thro' every age of their fcornful Phillis's——You never knew a bold fellow, who could love Women without miftaking 'em for Angels, whine about their cruelty.

Sir Ch. Do you not tell me your Sifter's heart is engaged ? —Then what have I to ftruggle for ? it was her heart I wifh'd to poffefs. Could Mifs Hargrave be indelicate enough, which I am fure fhe could not, to beftow her hand on me without it, I would reject it.

Geo. Bravo!—nobly refolved ! keep it up by all means,—— Come now, I'll introduce you to one of the fineft Girls you ever faw in your life—but remember you are not to fuffer your heart to be interefted there, for that's my quarry—and death to the man who attempts to rob me of my prize !

Sir Ch. Oh, you are very fecure, I affure you—my heart is adamant from this moment.   [*Exeunt.*

The Garden. Enter HARGRAVE *and a* Servant.

Mr. Har. Run and tell my Son I want to fpeak to him here directly [*exit Serv.*] Her forty thoufand pounds will juft enable me to buy the Greenwood Eftate,—and to my certain knowledge, that young Rakehelly won't be able to keep it to his back much longer. We fhall then have more land than any family in the country, and a Borough of our own into the bargain. Humph—But fuppofe George fhould not have a mind to marry her now ? Why then,—why then—as to his mind, when two parties differ, the weaker muft give way—the match is for the advancement of your fortune, fays I ; and if it can't fatisfy your mind, you muft teach it what I have always taught you—obedience.——[*Enter* GEO.]

Oh, George, I fent for you into the garden, that we might have no interruptions ; for, as I was faying, there's an affair of confequence I want to talk to you about.

Geo. I am all attention, Sir.

Mr. H. I don't defign that you fhall return to College any more—I have other views, which I hope will not be difagreeable to you—You— you like Lady Dinah, you fay ?.

Geo. [*hefitatingly*] She is a Lady of great erudition, without doubt.

Mr. H. I don't know what your notions may be of her age ; I could wifh her a few years younger, but——

Geo. Pardon me, Sir, I think there can be no objection to her age ; and the preference her Ladyfhip gives to our family, is certainly a high compliment.

Mr. H. Ho, ho, then you are acquainted already with what I was going to communicate to you——I am furprifed at that.

Geo. Matrimonial negotiations, Sir, are feldom long concealed ; 'tis a fubject on which every body is fond of talking— the young, in hopes that their turn will come ;—and thofe who are older——

Mr. H. By way of giving a fillip to their memories, I fuppofe you mean, George, eh ?—well, I am glad you are fo merry ; I was a little uneafy about what you might think of this affair—tho' I never mention'd it in my life—but perhaps, Lady Dinah may have hinted it to her woman, and then I fhould not wonder if the whole parifh knew it. However, you have no objection, and that's enough—tho' if you had, I muft have had my way, George.

Geo. Without doubt, Sir.

Mr. H. Have you fpoken to Lady Dinah on the fubject ?

Geo. Spoke— n - - o, Sir, I could not think of addreffing Lady Dinah on fo delicate an affair without your permiffion.

Mr. H. Well then, my dear Boy—I would have you fpeak to her now, and, I think, the fooner the better.

Geo. To be fure, Sir—I fhall obey you—

Mr. H. Well, you have fet my heart at reft——I am as happy as a Prince—I never fixt my mind on any thing in my life, fo much as I have done on this marriage—and it would have gall'd me forely if you had been againft it—but you are a good Boy, George, a very good Boy, and I'll go in, and prepare Lady Dinah for your vifit. [*Exit.*

Geo. Why, my dear Father, you are quite elated on the profpect of your nuptials—but why muft *I* make fpeeches to Lady Dinah ? I am totally ignorant of the mode that elderly Gentlemen adopt on fuch occafions.

Enter BELLA.

Bel. What, have you been opening your heart to your Father, George?

Geo. No, faith—he has been opening his to me—He has been making me the confident of his paſſion for Lady Dinah.

Bel. No! ha, ha, ha—is it poſſible?—what ſtyle does he talk in? is it flames and darts, or eſteem and ſentiment?

Geo. I don't imagine my good Father thinks of either— her fortune, I preſume, is his objeƈt; and I ſhall not venture to hint an objeƈtion; for contradiƈtion, you know, only lends him freſh ardor. Where is Seymour and Harriet?

Bel. Your Siſter is in the drawing-room, and Sir Charles I juſt now ſaw in the Orange-walk, with his arms folded thus—and his eyes fixt on a ſhrub, in the moſt *penſeroſo* ſtyle you can conceive—Why—he has no appearance of a happy youth on the verge of Bridegroomiſm.

Geo. Ha, ha, ha, ha!

Bel. Why do you laugh?

Geo. At the embarraſment I have thrown the ſimpletons into—ha, ha, ha!

Bel. What ſimpletons?—what embarraſment?

Geo. That you cannot gueſs, my ſweet Couſin, with all your penetration.

Bel. I ſhall expire, if you won't let me know it—now do—pray, George—come—be pleas'd to tell it me. [*curtſeying.*

Geo. No, no, you look ſo pretty while you are coaxing, that I muſt—muſt ſee you in that humour a little longer.

Bel. That's unkind—come—tell me this ſecret—tho' I'll be hang'd if I don't gueſs it.

Geo. Nay, then I muſt tell you; for if you ſhou'd find it out, I ſhall loſe the pleaſure of obliging you.—Seymour and my Siſter doat on one another—and I have made each believe, that the other has different engagements.

Bel. Oh, I am rejoiced to hear it.

Geo. Rejoic'd! I aſſure you, I am highly offended.

Bel. At what? Sir Charles is your friend, and every way an eligible match for your Siſter.

Geo. Very true——I am happy in their attachment, and therefore offended.——Sir Charles has been as chary of his ſecret, as if I had not deſerv'd his confidence.

Bel. I believe he never addreſs'd your Siſter.

Geo. Aye, ſo he pretends, he never made love to her—— ridiculous ſubterfuge!—he ſtole into her heart by the help of thoſe ſilent tender obſervances, which are the ſureſt battery when there's time to play 'em off——If any man had *thus* obtain'd my Siſter's heart——left her a prey to diſappointment, and then faid—*he meant nothing*—my fword fhould have taught him, that his conduct was not lefs difhonourable, than if he had knelt at her feet, and fworn a million oaths.

Bel. Why, this might be ufeful——but, mercy upon us! if every girl had fuch a fnap-dragon of a Brother,—no Beaus —and very few pretty fellows would venture to come near her—pray, when did you form this mifchievous defign?

Geo. Oh, Sir Charles has been heaping up the meafure of his offences fome time—'twould have diverted you to have feen the tricks he play'd to get Harriet's picture——At laft he begg'd it, to get the drapery copied for his Sifter's; and I know 'tis at this moment in his bofom, tho' he has fworn an hundred times 'tis ftill at the Painter's.

Bel. Ha!—I'll fly and tell her the news——If I don't miftake, fhe'd rather have her picture there than in the Gallery of Beauties at Hampton. [*going.*]

Geo. Sdeath!—ftop—Why, are not you angry?—fhut out by parchment provifoes from all the flutters of Courtfhip yourfelf—you had a right to participate in Harriet's.

Bel. Very true; this might be fufficient for *me*——But what pleafure can *you* have in tormenting two hearts fo attach'd to each other?

Geo. I do mean to plague 'em a little; and it will be the greateft favour we can do them—for they are fuch fentimental people—you know—that they'll blufh, and hefitate, and torment each other, fix months before they can come to an explanation——But, by alarming their jealoufy, they'll betray themfelves in as many hours.

Bel. Oh, cry your mercy!—So there's not one grain of mifchief in all this; and you carry on the plan in downright charity—well, really in that light there is fome reafon—

Geo. Aye, more reafon than is neceffary to induce you to join in it—even tho' there were mifchief—fo promife me your affiftance with a good grace.

Bel. Well, I do promife; for I really think——

Geo. Oh, I'll accept of very flight affurances.

Bel. A-propos! Here's Harriet—I'm juft as angry as you wifh me: leave us, and you fhall have a good account of her.

Enter HARRIET.

Har. Brother! Mr. Drummond, I fancy, wonders at your abfence: he's alone with the Lady——

Geo. Then he poffeffes a privilege that half mankind would grudge him.   [*Exit.*

Bel. Have you feen Sir Charles yet?

E

Har. Indeed I have not—I confeſs I was ſo weak, as to
retire twice from the drawing-room, becauſe I heard his voice
—tho' I was conſcious my abſence muſt appear odd, and
fearful the cauſe might be ſuſpected.

Bel. Ah !—pray be careful that you give *him* in particu-
lar no reaſon to gueſs at that—I adviſe you to treat him with
the greateſt coldneſs.

Har. Moſt certainly I ſhall, whatever it coſts me——It
would be the moſt cruel mortification, if I thought he would
ever ſuſpect my weakneſs—I wonder, Bella, if the Lady
whom he is to marry, is ſo handſome as George deſcribes her.

Bel. Of what conſequence is that to you, child ?—never
think about it ; if you ſuffer your mind to be ſoften'd with
reflections of that ſort, you'll never behave with a proper de-
gree of ſcorn to him.

Har. Oh, do not fear it ; I aſſure you, I poſſeſs a vaſt
deal of ſcorn for him.

Bel. I am ſure you fib, [*aſide.*]—Well now, by way of
example, he is coming this way, I ſee.

Har. Is he ?—come then, let us go.

Bel. Yes, yes, you are quite a Heroine, I perceive——
Surely you will not fly to prove your indifference ?—Stay
and mortify him with an appearance of careleſsneſs and good-
humour——For inſtance : when he appears, look at him with
ſuch an unmeaning eye, as one glances over an acquaintance
ſhabbily dreſs'd at Ranelagh—and when he ſpeaks to you,
look another way ; and then, ſuddenly recollecting yourſelf,
—What is that you were ſaying, Sir Charles ? I beg pardon,
I really did not attend—then, without minding his anſwer—
Bella, I was thinking of that ſweet fellow who open'd the
ball with Lady Harriet—Did you ever ſee ſuch eyes ? and
then the air with which he danced !—O Lord ! I never ſhall
forget him.

Har. You'll find me a bad ſcholar, I believe—however,
I'll go through the interview, if you'll aſſiſt me.

Bel. Fear me not.

Enter Sir CHARLES.

Sir Cha. Ladies—this is rather unexpected—I hope I
don't intrude.

Bel. Sir Charles Seymour can never be an unwelcome in-
truder.

Sir Cha. Miſs Hargrave—I have not had the happineſs
of paying my reſpects to you ſince I arriv'd—I hope you have
enjoyed a perfect ſhare of health and ſpirits, ſince I left Har-
grave-Place. [*confuſedly.*]

Har. I never have been better, Sir ; and my spirits are seldom so good as they are now. [*affecting gaiety.*]

Sir Cha. Your looks indeed, Madam, speak you in possession of that happiness I wish you [*sighing*]—You, Miss Sydney, are always in spirits.

Bel. In general, Sir—I have not wisdom enough to be troubled with reflections to destroy my repose.

Sir Cha. Do you imagine it then a proof of wisdom to be unhappy ?

Bel. One might think so ; for wise folks are always grave.

Har. Then I'll never attempt to be wise—henceforward I'll be gaiety itself—I am determined to devote myself to pleasure, and only live to laugh.

Bel. Perhaps you may not always find subjects, Cousin, unless you do as I do—laugh at your own absurdities.

Har. Oh, fear not—we need not always look at home ; the world abounds with subjects for mirth, and the men will be so obliging as to furnish a sufficient number, when every other resource fails.

Sir Cha. Miss Hargrave was not always so severe.

Har. Fye, Sir Charles—do not mistake pleasantry for severity——but exuberant spirits frequently overflow in impertinence ; therefore I pardon your thinking that mine do.

Sir Cha. Impertinence ! Surely, Madam, you cannot suppose I meant to———

Har. Nay, Bella, I appeal to you ; did not Sir Charles intimate some such thing ?

Bel. Why—a—I don't know——To be sure there was a kind of a distant intimation—tho' perhaps Sir Charles only means that you are aukward—ha ! ha !——But consider, Sir, this character of Harriet's is but lately assumed—and new characters, like new stays, never fit till they have been worn.

Sir Cha. Very well, Ladies ; I will not dispute your right to understand my expressions in what manner you please —but I hope you will allow me the same—and that, when a Lady's eyes speak disdain, I may, without offence, translate it into Love.

Har. 'Tis an error that men are apt to fall into ; but the eyes talk in an idiom, warm from the heart ; and so skilful an observer as Sir Charles will not mistake their language.

Sir Cha. Are they alike intelligible to all ?

Har. So plain, that nine times out of ten, at least, mistakes must be wilful.

E 2

Sir Ch. Then pray examine mine, Madam, and by the report you make I shall judge of your proficiency in their dialect.

Bella. Oh—I'll examine yours, Sir Charles—I am a better judge than Harriet—let me see—aye—'tis so, in one I perceive love and jealousy—in the other, hope and a wedding. Now am I not a Prophetess?

Sir Ch. Prove but one in the last article, and I ask no more of Fate—now—will *you* read? Madam!

Har. You are so intirely satisfied with Bella's translation, Sir, that I will not run the risk of mortifying you with a different construction—come, Cousin—let us return to our company.

Bel. [apart] Fye! that air of pique is enough to ruin all.

Sir Ch. Do you not find the garden agreeable, Miss Hargrave? I begin to think it charming.

Har. Perfectly agreeable, Sir—but the happy never fly society—I wonder to see you alone. Come, Bella.

Bel. Bravo!   *[Exeunt* Bella *and* Harriet.

Sir Ch. Astonishing! What is become of that sweetness—that dove-like softness, which stole into my heart, and deceived me into dreams of bliss? She flies from me, and talks of her company, and returning to her society—Oh Harriet! oh my Harriet! thy society is prized by me beyond that of the whole world; and still to possess it, with the hope that once glowed in my bosom, would be a blessing for which I would sacrifice every other, that Nature or Fortune has bestowed.   *[Exit.*

END OF THE SECOND ACT.

※※※※※※※※※※※※※※※※※※※※※※※

A C T III.

SCENE, *Lady* DINAH's *Dressing Room.*

Lady DINAH *and Mr.* HARGRAVE *sitting.*

Mr. Hargrave.

I AM surprised, Madam, at your thinking in this manner—when I spoke to my Son this morning—I assure you, he express'd a great deal of satisfaction about the affair—I wonder indeed he has not been here.

Lady D. Now, I could almoſt blame you, Mr. Hargrave —pardon me—but you have certainly been too precipitate— your Son has ſcarcely been at home four and twenty hours, and cannot poſſibly have received any impreſſion, or formed an idea of my charaƈter.—He has been ſo much engaged, in- deed, with other perſons, that I have had no opportunity of converſing with him ; and how, ſo circumſtanced, can he have form'd a judgment of his own heart ?

Mr. H. Good God ! Madam, he has given the beſt proof in the world that he has formed a judgment ; for he told me this morning, that the proſpeƈt of the marriage made him very happy.—I don't know what other proof a man can give that he knows his own heart—and let me tell you, Madam, I have accuſtomed my children to pay a proper regard to my inclination.

Lady D. I am apprehenſive, Sir, that Mr. George Har- grave's obedience may influence him more than I cou'd wiſh— and I aſſure you, I cannot think of uniting myſelf to any man, who does not prefer me for my own ſake, without ad- verting to any other conſideration.

Mr. H. His obedience to me, influence him more than you could wiſh !—why really I don't underſtand you, my Lady——Zounds ! I thought ſhe had been a ſenſible Wo- man. [aſide.

Lady D. Not underſtand me, Mr. Hargrave ! I have too high an opinion of your good ſenſe, to ſuppoſe that I am un- intelligible to you.

Mr. H. My opinion, Madam, is, that an obedient Son is likely to make a kind Huſband—George is a fine young fel- low as any in England, though I his father ſay it,—and there's not a woman in the kingdom, who might not be proud to call him her Huſband—too obedient—

Lady D. Bleſs me ! this man has no ideas [aſide.]—You miſtake me, Mr. Hargrave ; I do not mean to leſſen the merit of obedience in your Son—but, I confeſs, I wiſh him to have a more delicate, a more tender motive, for offering his hand to me.

Mr. H. Look ye, Madam—you have a great under- ſtanding, to be ſure——and I confeſs you talk above my reach—but I muſt nevertheleſs take the liberty to blame your Ladyſhip ;—a perſon of your Ladyſhip's experience—and, al- low me to ſay, your date in the world, muſt know that there are occaſions in which we ſhould not be too nice.

Lady D. Too nice ! Mr. Hargrave—— [riſing.

Mr. H. Aye—too nice, my Lady,—a Boy and Girl of fixteen, have time before 'em—they may be whimfical, and be off and on, and play at fhilly-fhally as long as they have a mind.—But, my Lady, at a certain feafon we muft leave off thefe tricks, or be content to go to the grave old Batchelors and—— *[fhrugging his fhoulders.*

Lady D. I am utterly aftonifhed, Mr. Hargrave——you furely mean to offend me—you infult me.

Mr. H. No—by no means——I would not offend your Ladyfhip for the world——I have the higheft refpect for you, and fhall rejoice to call you my Daughter—if you are not fo, it will be your own fault—for George, I am fure, is ready the moment you will give your confent—The writings fhall be drawn when you think proper, and the marriage confummated without delay.

Lady D. Well, Sir—I really do not know what to fay—when Mr. George Hargrave fhall imagine it a proper period to talk to me on the fubject—I—I—

Mr. H. Well, well, Madam—I allow this is a topic on which a Lady does not chufe to explain herfelf but to the principal——I waited on your Ladyfhip only to inform you that I had talked to my Son concerning the affair, and to incline you, when he waits on you, to give him a favourable hearing.

Lady D. Mr. Hargrave—a perfon of your Son's merit is *entitled* to a proper attention from any Woman he addreffes.

Mr. H. There—now we are right again—I was fearful that you had not liked my Boy——and that your difficulties arofe from that quarter——but fince you like George, 'tis all very well, very well.

Lady D. Mr. Hargrave!——I am furprifed at your conceiving fo unjuft an idea ——Mr. George Hargrave is, as you have faid, a match for any woman, whatever be her rank.

Mr. H. My dear Lady Dinah—I am quite happy to hear you fay fo—I am fure George loves *you*—odds bobs, I hear him on the ftairs——I'll go and fend him to you this moment, and he fhall tell you fo himfelf——you'll furely believe *him.*
[Exit.

Lady D. Mr. Hargrave, Mr. Hargrave—blefs me, what an impetuous obftinate old Man—what can I do?——I am in an exceedingly indelicate fituation——he will tell his Son that I am waiting here in expectation of a declaration of love from him—Sure never woman was in fo aukward an embarras—I *wifh* the Son poffeffed a little of the Father's impetuofity—this would not then have happened.

Enter GEORGE.

Geo. Your Ladyſhip's moſt obedient ſervant.

Lady D. S -- i -- r [*curtſeying confuſedly*]

Geo. My Father permits me, Madam, to make my acknowledgments to your Ladyſhip, for the honour you deſign
our Family.

Lady D. I muſt confeſs, Sir, this interview is ſomewhat
unexpected—it is indeed quite premature—I was not prepared
for it, and I am really in great confuſion.

Geo. I am ſenſible, Madam, a viſit of this kind to a Lady
of your delicacy muſt be a little diſtreſſing—but I intreat you
to be compoſed——I hope you will have no reaſon to regret a
reſolution which myſelf, and the reſt of the family, have ſo
much cauſe to rejoice in—and I aſſure your Ladyſhip, every
thing on my part, that can contribute to your felicity, you
ſhall always command.

Lady D. You are very *polite*, Sir—We have had ſo little
opportunity of converſing, Mr. Hargrave, that I am afraid
you expreſs rather your Father's ſentiments than your own.
It is impoſſible, indeed, from ſo ſhort a knowledge, that you
can have formed any ſentiments of me yourſelf.

Geo. Pardon me, Madam, my ſentiments for you are full
of reſpect—and I am convinced your qualities will excite the
veneration of all who have the honour of being connected with
you. My Father could hardly have done it better. [*aſide.*]

Lady D. Why, this young Man has certainly been taught
to make love by his Tutor at College. [*aſide.*]

Geo. I am concerned this viſit ſeems ſo embarraſſing to
your Ladyſhip—I certainly ſhould have deferr'd it, from an
apprehenſion of its being diſagreeable, but, in obedience to
my Father, I—

Lady D. Then it is to your Father, Sir, that I am indebted for the favour of ſeeing you.

Geo. By no means, Madam—it would certainly have
been my *inclination* to have waited on your Ladyſhip, but
my Father's wiſhes induced me to haſten it.

Lady D. Really! a pretty extraordinary confeſſion! [*aſide.*]
—I think it neceſſary to aſſure you, Sir, that—that this affair has been brought thus forward by Mr. Hargrave——and
the propoſals he made, in which it was evident, *his whole heart*
was concern'd, were quite unexpected.

Geo. I have not the leaſt doubt of it, Madam, nor am I
at all ſurpriſed at my Father's earneſtneſs, on a ſubject ſo intereſting—What can ſhe mean by apologizing to me? [*aſide*]

Lady D. It would certainly have been proper, Sir, to have allowed you time to have formed a judgment yourself, on a point which coucerns you so highly.

Geo. The time has been quite sufficient, Madam—I highly approve the steps my Father has taken—but if I did not, the respect I bear to his determination would certainly have prevented my opposing them. I must end this extraordinary visit [*aside.*]—Shall I have the honour of conducting your Ladyship to the Company?

Lady D. N -- o, Sir—I have some orders to give my Woman, I'll rejoin the Ladies in a few minutes.

Geo. Then I'll wish your Ladyship a good morning. [*Ex.*

Lady D. Amazement! why, what a visit from a Lover! ——Is this the language in which men usually talk to women, with whom they are on the point of marriage?———— Respect! Veneration! Obedience to my Father!—And shall I have the honour of conducting your Ladyship to the Company?—A pretty Lover-like request truly!——But this coldness to me proceeds from a cause I now understand——This morning, what fire was there in his eyes! what animation in his countenance! whenever he address'd himself to that creature Mr. Drummond brought here?—Would his request to her have been to conduct her to Company?—No, no;— But I must be cautious——I must be patient now—but you will find, Sir, when I possess the privileges of a Wife, I shall not so easily give them up—your fiery glances, if not directed to me, shall at least, in my presence, be addressed to no other.
[*Exit.*

SCENE *changes to an Apartment.*

BELLA *at her Harpsichord.*

S O N G.

Haste, haste, ye fiery Steeds of Day,
   In Ocean's bosom hide your beams!
Mild Evening, in her pensive gray
   More soft, and more alluring seems.

Yet why invoke the pensive Eve,
   Or, sighing, chide refulgent Morn?
Their shifting moments can't relieve
   The heart by pangs of absence torn.

Hang Music——it only makes me melancholy——Heigh-ho!——these Lovers infect me too, I believe——Seducive Italy! what are your attractions? Oh, for Fortunatus's cap—I'd convince myself in a moment if my doubts are

juftly founded——And fuppofe they fhould——what then?—
Ah! they think I am made of ice, whilft the gaiety of my
difpofition only ferves to conceal a heart as tenderly fufceptible
as the moft ferious of my fex can poffefs——

Enter EMILY.

Ah, my dear Ma'am, I am rejoiced to fee you; I have been
juft long enough alone to be tired of myfelf, and to be charmed
at fo agreeable a relief.

Em. Can that ever be the cafe with Mifs Sidney? I
thought you had poffefs'd the happieft flow of fpirits in the
world.

Bel. Pho!—your great fpirits are mere Jack-a-lanterns
in the brain—they dance about, fhine, and make vagaries
—while thofe who poffefs happinefs, *foberly* and quietly enjoy their treafure.

Em. Indeed! I hope *dulnefs* is not your criterion of
happinefs—if it is, there are few affemblies where you'll not
find a great number to envy.

Bel. Oh, no——Dulnefs is the character of thofe who are
too wife, not too happy.

Enter GEORGE.

Geo. Two Ladies in council—on fafhion, or news?

Bel. On a better fubject—laughing at the flaves we have
made, and forging chains for more.

Geo. That's not the bufinefs of fine Women—
Nature meant to fave them the trouble of plotting—for
traps and chains, fhe beftowed fparkling eyes, and timid
blufhes, with a whole multitude of graces, that hang about
the form, and wanton in the air. [*Looking at* Emily.]

Bel. Well, after all, Men are delightful creatures—flattery, cards, and fcandal, help one thro' the day tolerably
well—I don't know how we fhould exift without 'em in the
country.

Geo. And which of 'em would you relinquifh in town?

Bel. Not flattery, becaufe it keeps one in fpirits, and
gives a glow to the complexion——Scandal, you may take
away—but pray leave us cards, to keep us awake, with the
fafhionable world, on Sunday evenings.

Geo. And, in lieu of fcandal, you'll be content with conqueft.

Bel. Ridiculous! Conqueft is not fuch an object with Women, as the Men imagine—for my part, I fhould conceive a
net that would catch the hearts of the whole fex, a property
of very little value.

F

Geo. But, you would think it a very pleafant one, my gentle Cuz. or, at leaft [*archly*] you'd pick out one happy favourite before you gave the reft to defpair.

Bel. Pofitively no——I don't know one that I fhould not let fly away with the reft.

Geo. Now, how can you fib, with fuch an unblufhing face? This debate, Madam, [*to Emily*] will let you into Bella's fecret—fhe has, at this moment, an image in her heart, that gives a flat contradiction to her tongue.

Bel. Indeed!—you make your affertion with great effrontery——but now, to compliment your difcernment, whofe image do you think of?

Geo. Ha, Bella——liften with your greedieft ears to catch the tranfporting found—breathe not, ye fofteft Zephyrs! be filent, ye harmonious Spheres! while I articulate the name of——

Bel. [*ftopping her ears*] Oh, I won't hear it.

Geo. Belville!

Bel. Oh, frightful!—don't attend to him—George's belief is always under the influence of his fancy.

Emily. In this inftance, if I may judge from your looks, he has not hinted at a fiction.

Bel. Indeed you are miftaken; his guefs might have been as good, if you had named Prefter John.

Geo. Hum—I wifh it may be fo, for I have heard a ftory about a certain Lady on the Continent, whom a certain Gentleman—

Bel. Thinks handfomer than Bella Sydney—mortifying—ha, ha, ha!

Geo. Nay more, to whom he devotes his hours.

Bel. His heart [*petulantly.*]

Geo. On whom he doats.

Bel. Pfha!

Geo. Grows melancholy.

Bel. Nonfenfe!

Geo. Nay, fights for her.

Bel. Ridiculous!

Geo. Lives only at her feet.

Bel. You are really very infupportable, Sir—do find fome other fubject to amufe yourfelf.

Geo. Ha, ha, ha! the Gudgeon has bit—See, Madam, a Coquette ftruggling with the confcioufnefs of love,—are not thofe pouts, and angry blufhes, proofs of Belville's happinefs?

Emily. I cannot perceive thefe proofs—Mr. Belville, perhaps, is not in fo enviable a ftate.

Bel. Oh, you are a good Girl, and, I affure you, perfectly right—Lovers, thank our ftars! are too plenty, for an ab-fent one to give us much pain.—What, turn your arms on your affociate, George!—I'll break the league, and difcover all. [*apart to* George.

Geo. You dare not, you love mifchief too well—it is as dear to you as the fighs of your Lover.

Bel. A-propos! where's Sir Charles?

Geo. In the garden probably—fighing to the winds—and I wifh you'd find him—and leave us. [*apart.*

Bel. Ha! Perhaps they'll waft his fighs to Harriet—and fhe muft not hear 'em yet—and fo, Sir Charles— [*Exit.*

Emily. Oh, pray make me one of your party. [*going.*

Geo. Stay, Madam, I entreat you—believe me, they will not thank you—I'll tell you the ftory.

Emily. I'll hear it from Mifs Sydney.

Geo. Nay, if you are determined— [*Exeunt.*

SCENE, *the Garden.*

Enter HARRIET.

In vain do I endeavour to conceal it from myfelf—This fpot has charms for me, that I can find in no other——here have I feen—perhaps for the laft time, Sir Charles Seymour. My Coufin's prefence was unlucky—I fhould have heard him —but it would have been a crime in him to have talked to me of love—an infult that I muft have refented—and yet 'tis the only fubject on which I could wifh to have heard him. Blefs me! he's here again—he haunts this place—but he does not obferve me, and I'll conceal myfelf; for I feel I could not now behave with proper referve. [*Goes behind an arbor.*

Enter Sir CHARLES, *looking round.*

Ha, not here then!—Sweet *refemblance* of her I love! come from thy hiding-place. [*takes a picture from his bofom, and kiffes it.*] In her abfence thou art the deareft object to my eyes. What a face is this!

" 'Tis beauty truly bleft, whofe red and white
" Nature's own fweet and cunning hand laid on."

Enter GEORGE. *Catches his hand with the picture.*

Geo. Ho ho!—fo the Picture's come home from the Painter's, is it, Sir—and the drapery quite to your mind?

Sir Ch. [*confufed and recovering.*] The artifice I ufed to obtain it, thofe who love can pardon.

Geo. And how many times a day doft thou break the decalogue in worfhipping that Image ?

Sir Ch. Every hour that I live. I gaze on it till I think it looks, and fpeaks to me ; it lies all night on my heart, and is the firft objeft I addrefs in the morning.

Geo. Oh, complete your charaĉter, and turn Monk— 'tis plain you're half a Papift.

Sir Ch. Why condemn me to cells and penitence ?

Geo. That you mayn't violate the laws of Nature, by pretending to a charaĉter for which fhe never defigned you. Your bonds, inftead of filken fetters, appear to be hempen cords. Come, confefs, have not you been examining on which of thefe trees you would be moft gracefully pendent?

Sir Ch. That *gaieté de cœur*, George, bears no mark of the tender paffion ; and, to be plain, I believe you know very little about it.

Geo. You are confoundedly miftaken—we are both Lovers, but the difference between us lies thus : Cupid to me is a little familiar rogue, with an arch leer—and cheeks dimpled with continual fmiles—To you—an aweful Deity, deck'd out in his whole regalia of darts, flames, and quivers, and fo forth—I play with him—you———

Sir Ch. Spare yourfelf the trouble of fo long an explanation—All you would fay is, that you love with hope—I with defpair.

Geo. Very concife, and moft pathetically expreft— melancholy fuits your features, Charles—'twere pity your Miftrefs fhould encourage you ; it would deprive you of that *fomething* in your air which is fo touching—Ha ! ha ! ha !—poor Seymour ! Come, let us go in fearch of the girls, they are gone to the wood ; who knows but you may find a nymph there, who'll have the kindnefs to put hanging and drowning out of your head ?

Sir Ch.   Oh, would fweet Celia meet me there,
        With foften'd looks, and gentler air,
        Tranfported, to the Wood I'd fly,
        The happieft Swain beneath the fky ;
        Sighs and complaints I'd give the wind,
        And IO's fing, were Celia kind.

[*As he repeats the verfes,* George, *laughing, fcans them on his fingers.*   [*Exit Sir* Charles.

Geo. Cupid is deaf, as well as blind. [*Exit* George.

Enter HARRIET.

Har. Her picture in his bosom, and kiss it with such rapture too ! Well—I am glad I am convinced—I am perfectly at ease. ' He loves them without hope, and George was mistaken in supposing him so near marriage—but he loves notwithstanding—her picture lies all night on his heart, and her idea is never absent from his mind——Well, be it so—I am perfectly at ease, and shall no longer find a difficulty in assuming an indifference that is become real——Oh, Seymour! [*Exit.*

S C E N E, *the Wood.*

Enter Lady DINAH.

Insolent wretch !——Nothing less than the conviction of my own senses could have induced me to believe so shocking an indecorum——I saw her myself look at him with eyes that were downright gloting——I saw him snatch her hand, and press it to his lips, with an ardour that is inconceivable—and when the creature pretended to blush, and made a reluctant effort to withdraw it—*my* Youth, so full of veneration and respect for me, refused to resign it—till the creature had given him a gracious smile of reconciliation——Heavens! they are coming this way—sure they do not perceive me—See there !—Nay, if you will come here. [*Goes behind a shrub.*]

Enter EMILY, *followed by* GEORGE.

Em. I entreat you, Sir, not to persist in following me—You'll force me to appeal to Mr. Drummond for protection.

Geo. You need no protection, Madam, that you will not find in my respect—But you are barbarous to deprive me of conversing with you—'tis a felicity, I have so lately tasted, that 'tis no wonder I am greedy of it.

Em. If you believe your attentions would not displease me in my proper character—I ought to be offended that you address them to a person, of whose name and family you are ignorant.

Geo. Can a name deprive you of that face, that air—or rob you of your mind—of what then am I ignorant ?—'tis those I address with the most passionate vows of——

Em. I positively will not listen to you——However, if the acquaintance should place us on a footing, I'll then

converfe with you—if on my own terms. [*Lady* D. *liften-*
ing—Aye, or on any terms.] I have no diflike to the
charming freedom of the Englifh manners—you fhall be as
gallant as you pleafe ; but I give you notice, the inftant
you become dangerous, I fhall be grave.

Geo. How dangerous———

Em. Oh, the moment you grow of confequence enough
to endanger my heart, I fhall fhut myfelf from you—but
as long as you continue harmlefs, you may play.

Geo. This is not to be borne—I will not be harmlefs—
I declare open war againft your heart, not in play, but
downright earneft.

Em. Nay, then, I muft colleél my forces to oppofe
you—my heart will ftand a long fiege, depend on it.

Geo. If you'll promife it fhall yield at laft, a ten years
fiege will be richly rewarded.

Em. Oh, no ; I make no promifes—try your forces ; if
you fhould poffefs yourfelf of it in fpite of me—I can only
bewail its captivity.

Geo. Your permiffion to take the field is all I can at
prefent hope ; and thus on my knees, dear charming Creature———

Lady D. [*liftening*] There's veneration and refpeét !

Em. Hold, Sir—I will be fo generous to tell you, that
whenever you kneel I fhall fly. [*runs out.*]

Geo. And I'll purfue—till my Atalanta confeffes I have
won the prize. [*As* Geo. *is following* Emily, *Lady* D.
*comes out againft him with an angry reprpachful air, and paffes
him.*]

Geo. [*afide*] So,—there's a look! what a bleffed Mother-
in-law I fhall have !   [*Exit.*

Lady D. What !—not ftay even to explain—to apolo-
gife—follow her before my face—oh, Monfters, Furies !
yes, yes, fhe'll yield without the trouble of a ten years
fiege—fhe can fcarcely hold out ten minutes—oh, ye fhall
both fuffer for this—I will go this inftant—I will do fomething.   [*Exit,*

Enter SUSAN.

Sufan. Hah, my good Lady, is it fo ? ha, ha, ha! I muft
fee if I can't make myfelf ufeful here. A Lady, who like my
miftrefs gives way to her moft unbridled paffions, is the only
one worth being ferved by a girl of fpirit and intrigue. I'll
follow, and aid your Ladyfhip with my counfel before you

have time to cool—[*going, 'returns.*]—So—'tis needlefs, here
fhe ebbs, like a ftormy fea.

Enter Lady DINAH, *not feeing* SUSAN.

Lady D. A moment's reflection has convinced me I fhould
be wrong—he muft not fufpect that I influence his Father
againft the minion—nor will I allow her the fatisfaction of
thinking fhe gives to me the pangs of jealoufy—but I will not
lofe him—fomething muft be done.

Sufan. Oh, my Lady, I was witnefs to the whole affair—
Oh, a bafe man! I could have trampled him under my feet.

Lady D. Bafe, indeed! but 'tis on *her* my refentment
chiefly falls—oh, Sufan—revenge!

Sufan. I am fure my heart achs for you, my Lady—there's
nothing I would not do—Oh, fhe's an artful flut.

Lady D. She's as dangerous as artful—· I muft be rid of
· her, yet I know not how.—Oh France! for thy Baftile, for
· thy *Lettres de Cachet* !

· *Sufan.* There are ways and means here, my Lady—Mifs
· told a fine tale to get into the houfe, and I fancy I can tell as
· fine a tale to get her out of it, and I fhou'd think it neither
· fin nor fhame in the fervice of fo good a Lady.

Lady D. If thou canft contrive any method—I care not
what—any plan to rid me of her; command my fortune.

Sufan. Oh, dear my Lady, as to that—as to your fortune,
my Lady, that's out of the queftion—but I know your Ladyfhip's generofity—I think I could fend her packing,—perhaps
before night.

Lady D. Can you!—The inftant fhe goes, I'll give you
two hundred pounds.

Sufan. [*courtefying*] She fhall go, my Lady, if I have in-
vention, or Jarvis a tongue.

Lady D. Jarvis! Are you mad?—I wou'd not have him
fufpect that I am concerned in the affair, for the univerfe.

Sufan. Oh, dear my Lady—I vow I wou'd not mention
your name to him—no, not for another two hundred pounds;
—no, no, Mifs fhall be got rid of, without giving Jarvis, or
any one, the leaft reafon to fufpect that your Ladyfhip is privy
to the matter.

Lady D. I am convinced fhe is an impoftor, and I wonder
Mr. Hargrave doesn't fee it—but there will be more labour in
roufing his ftupid apprehenfion, than in explaining to an en-
thufiaft the conceptions of a Bolingbroke.

Sufan. I am more afraid of Mr. Drummond than him.

Lady D. Aye—he will fupport that Girl's intereft, in order to mortify me—

Sufan. That doesn't fignify, my Lady—I have a card as good as any he holds to play againft him—your Ladyfhip muft have feen that the old Juftice has full as much weight with the 'Squire, as Mr. Drummond.

Lady D. I obferve that Mr. Hargrave is continually wavering between them—they influence his actions like two principal fenfes—Mr. Drummond is the friend of his underftanding, the other of his humour.—But what is the card you mean to play?

Sufan. I mean to play one of his fenfes againft the other, my Lady, that's all—for I am miftaken if I can't govern the Juftice, as much as his whole five put together.

Lady. D. That is indeed a card—my hopes catch life at it—Sufan, fay to him what you will, promife what you will—I fuppofe you have the way to the old fool's heart, and know by what road to reach it—at all events the Girl muft be got rid of; the method I leave to you.—There's the dinner bell—I muft walk a little to recover my compofure, and then, I fuppofe, I may have the honour of fitting for the young Lady's foil.   [*Exit.*

Sufan. I am fure fhe can't have a better—ha, ha, ha!—Two hundred pounds! Oh the charms of jealoufy and revenge—I might have ferved one of your good fort of orderly old women, 'till I had been grey—thefe two hundreds will quicken Mr. Jarvis a little—we fhall fee him more attentive, I fancy, than he has been, and then farewell to fervitude—Hah, Jarvis!

Enter Jarvis *bowing affectedly.*

Jar. " So look'd the Goddefs of the Paphian Ifle,
      " When Mars fhe faw, and conquer'd with that fmile."
My dear Goddefs, I kifs your fingers—I have been hunting for you in every walk in the garden.

Sufan. [*tenderly*] Why—what did you want with me, Jarvis?

Jar. Why, faith, I have the fame kind of neceffity for you, that a Beau has for a looking-glafs——you admire me, and keep me in good humour with myfelf.

Sufan. Oh, if you want to be put in temper, I've got an excellent cordial. Now for your parts—now to prove yourfelf the clever fellow that you think you are.

Jar. That you think, my dear, you mean—but what ex-

Sufan. Liften!—We have difcovered that the young 'Squire thinks eighteen a prettier age than fifty—that he prefers natural rofes to Warren's, and that gravity and wifdom are no match for the fire of two hazel eyes, affifted by the reafoning of fmiles and dimples.

Jar. And he's in the right on't—didn't I tell you this morning they reckon'd without their hoft?

Sufan. Here has he been on his knees at the feet of the Damfel, and her Ladyfhip behind that bufh, amufing herfelf with his tranfports—ha, ha, ha!

Jar. Ha, ha, ha!—I warrant her, 'tis the only tranfports *fhe'll* ever fee him in. George Hargrave marry our old Lady! no, no—I have a very good opinion of that young fellow; he's exactly what I fhould be, if I was heir to his Father's acres—juft fuch a fpirited, carelefs deportment—a certain prevailing affurance—upon my foul, Sufan, you and I ought to have moved in a higher fphere.

Sufan. Come, come, you muft confider this affair in another light; 'twou'd be a fhame, that becaufe this Girl has a pretty face, and was found weeping by a compaffionate old Gentleman—it wou'd be a fhame, I fay, that for thefe reafons, fhe fhou'd marry into a great Family, and cheat the Sifter of a Peer, of a Hufband—Read the ftory *this* way, act with fpirit, and our Lady will, *on the day of our marriage*, give us two hundred pounds.

Jar. Humph!—on the day of our marriage—cannot you, Child, prevail on your Lady to give me the two hundred, without tacking that condition to it?

Sufan. Pho, Sauce-box!—Well, but thefe two hundreds now—what will you do for 'em?

Jar. Do for 'em—Oh, any thing—the moft extravagant thing in the world—run off with the girl—blow up the houfe—turn Turk—or marry you.

Sufan. Upon my word, Sir.

Jar. Well, but the bufinefs, Child, the bufinefs.

Sufan. The bufinefs is, that we muft contrive to open fome door for this Girl to walk out of the houfe.

Jar. But how—upon what ground—when, and where?

Sufan. Why, if we could contrive the bufinefs, I have no doubt of the fpirit and fire of your execution.—Do you remember the occupation which once gave employment to thefe talents of yours—I mean that of an itinerant Player?

Jar. Oh, yes—I remember the barns that I have made

G

echo with the ravings of Oreſtes, and the ſtables in which I
have ſighed forth the woes of Romeo.

Suſan. Well, but have you any recollection of a pretty
Juliet—a tall elegant Girl—in ſhort, do you not remember
one of the ſtrolling party exceedingly like the ſtrange gueſt
now in the houſe?

Jar. Hum !—Why, what devil ſent thee to tempt me
this morning ?—ſo I am to ſell my honour—my honeſty—

Suſan. Pho, pho—honeſty and honour are ſentiments for
people whoſe fortunes are made—let us once be independent,
and we'll be as honourable and as honeſt as the beſt of 'em—
ſo let's go in, and ſettle our plan.

Jar. Well—'tis the fate of great men to be in the hands
of Women ; and therefore, my ſweet Abigail—I am yours.
                                        [*Leads her off.*

END of the THIRD ACT.

✻✻✻✻✻✻✻✻✻✻✻✻✻✻✻✻✻✻✻✻✻✻✻✻✻✻✻✻✻

A C T   IV.

SCENE, *an Apartment.*

Enter HARRIET, *followed by* BELLA.

BELLA.

NAY, but hear him—hear him, Harriet.

Har. Can this be you, Bella, who this morning ſeem'd
fearful that I ſhould not treat him with ſufficient ſcorn—now
perſuading me to allow a private interview to a Man who is
profeſſedly the lover of another?

Bel. How apprehenſive you *very* delicate Ladies are!
Why muſt you ſuppoſe he wants to talk to you about love—
or on any topic, that his approaching marriage would make
improper ?

Har. Why—what *can* he have to ſay to me ?

Bel. Admit him, and he'll tell you—perhaps he wants to
conſult your taſte about the trimmings of his wedding clothes
—or to beg your choice in his ruffles—or—

Har. Pho !—this is downright ridicule.

Bel. Well then—you won't admit him ? [*ſeeming to go*] I
ſhall tell him you don't chooſe to ſee him, tho' he is going to

leave us directly——but I approve your caution, Harriet, you are perfectly right.

Har. Going to leave us directly, Bella!

Bel. Immediately, my dear——I heard him order his chaise, and mutter something about infupportable—but I think you'll be exceedingly imprudent in receiving his visit, and advise you by all means to refuse it.

Har. Dear Bella!

Bel. Well then you will see him——I shall acquaint him with the success of my embassy—but remember scorn, Harriet, scorn.   [*Exit Bella.*

Har. Now, what am I to expect? my heart beats strangely —but remember, foolish Girl, the picture of his Mistress is in his bosom.

Enter Sir CHARLES.

Sir Ch. The request I ventured to make by Miss Sidney, Madam, must appear strange to you—the engagements which I——

Har. Renders it an extraordinary request indeed, Sir.

Sir Cha. I fear'd you would think so, and conscious of those engagements, I shou'd not have presum'd to have made it—but as it's probably the last time I may ever see you—I seize it, to tell you that—I adore you.

Har. Sir Charles! I am astonished,—in my Father's house at least, I should have been secure from such an insult.

Sir Ch. Forgive me, I intreat you. Nothing could have forced this declaration from me, but my despair.

Har. The engagement you talk of, Sir, ought to have prevented *these* effects of your despair.

Sir Cha. I acknowledge it—and they have kept me silent ever since I arrived—but when I thought of leaving you in a few moments, I found the idea infupportable.

Har. The picture you wear, Sir Charles—might console you surely.

Sir Cha. Hah—I thought you were ignorant, Madam, of my possessing it.

Har. Without doubt you did, Sir Charles—but no, Sir— I am acquainted with your wearing that Picture—and wonder how you could presume—but I deserve the insult, for listening to you a moment.   [*Going.*

Sir Ch. Oh, stay, Miss Hargrave, I intreat you,—I will give up the picture, since it so offends you—yet how can I part from it?

G 2

Har. Oh, keep it, Sir——keep it by all means——you mistake me entirely, Sir ; I have no right to claim such a sacrifice. [*Going.*

Sir Ch. You have a right, Madam—here it is——[*kissing and offering it*] but do not rob me of it.

Har. Rob you of it !—in short, Sir Charles, you redouble your rudeness every moment—

Sir Ch. I did not think you would have so resented it— but I resign it to you, Madam—nay, you must take it.

Har. I take it, Sir ! [*Glances her eye on it, then takes it with an air of doubt*]——My Picture !——astonishing !

Enter GEORGE *and* BELLA, *both laughing.*

Sir Ch. Your picture, Madam ! !

Geo. Look at the simpletons—ha, ha, ha !

Bel. What a fine attitude !—do it again, Sir Charles— ha, ha, ha !—Well, Harriet—how do you like Sir Charles's Mistress ? Is she as handsome as George represented her ?

Geo. Hold, hold ! 'tis time now to have mercy. My dear Harriet, allow me to present to you my most valued friend, as the Man whom I should rejoice to see your Husband. To you, my Seymour, I present a Sister, whose heart has no engagements that I am acquainted with, to supersede your claim.

Sir Ch. I am speechless with joy, and with amazement.

Geo. Forgive the embarrasment I have occasion'd you— you have suffer'd something; but your felicity will be heighten'd from the comparison. My dear Harriet, Seymour has always loved you—the picture which so offended you is a proof, you cannot doubt.

Sir Ch. And that you were so offended, is supreme felicity—stupid wretch—not to perceive my bliss !

Har. [*to Geo. and Bel.*] You have taken a liberty with me that I cannot pardon.

Geo. Nay, but you shall pardon it—and as a proof, give him back your picture this minute.

Sir Ch. Return it to me, Madam, I intreat you [*kneeling*] I will receive it as the most precious gift.

Bel. Come, give the poor thing its bauble.

Har. Well, take it, Sir—since you had no share in this brilliant contrivance.

Sir Ch. [*taking the picture*] Eternal blessings on that hand !

Har. You, George, are never so happy, as in exercising your wit, at my expence.

Geo. And you, Harriet, never so heartily forgave me in your Life, and therefore——

Sir Ch. Hold, George—I cannot bear Miss Hargrave's suffering in this manner ; I will take on myself the transporting office of defending her—this hour, Madam, I shall for ever remember with gratitude, and will endeavour to deserve it, by a life devoted to your happiness.

Bel. Come, Harriet—I must take you away, that Sir Charles may bring down his raptures to the standard of common mortals—at present, I see his in the clouds.

Har. 'Tis merciful to relieve me.

[*Exeunt* Harriet *and* Bella.

Sir Ch. Charming Miss Sydney—I'll never quarrel with your vivacity again.——But why have I been made to suffer thus ?

Geo. Because you did not tell me *why* you wanted my Sister's picture—but I have taken a friendly vengeance ; my plot has told you more of my Sister's heart in a few hours, than all your sighs and humility, wou'd have obtained in as many months.

Sir Ch. For which I thank you—and my present happiness receives a brighter glow from this illusion of misery—I'll fly and pour out my joy and gratitude, at the feet of my charming Harriet. [*going. Enter* Bella.

Bel. Oh, stay, stay—we may want your assistance. Here's your Father coming, George. Your repartee to Lady Dinah at dinner, spoilt her digestion—and she's been representing you—that's all.

Geo. I hope she represented her sneer too, which suffused with tears the loveliest eyes in the world. Could I do less than support her against the ill-humour of that antiquated pedant ?—By Jupiter, I'll draw her in colours to my Father, that shall make him shrink from the fate he is preparing for himself.

Enter HARGRAVE.

Mr. H. Why, George, how's this ?—D'ye know what you've done?—you've affronted Lady Dinah.

Geo. I did not design to affront her, Sir—I only meant to convince her that she shou'd not insult the amiable young Lady, whom Mr. Drummond placed under your protection.

Mr. H. Don't tell me—amiable young Lady ! How do you know what she is ?—on the footing you are with Lady Dinah, let me tell you, if she had insulted an hundred young Ladies, you ought not to have seen it—at least, not resented it.

Geo. Pardon me, Sir—I did not conceive that Lady Dinah fhou'd have affumed in your houfe—at leaft till fhe becomes your Wife—a right to——

Mr. H. What's that you fay, Sir?

Geo. Indeed, Sir, to confefs the truth, I am aftonifh'd at your partiality for that Lady—fhe is the laft woman in the world, whom I could wifh to fee in the place of my amiable Mother.

Mr. H. Your Mother!

Geo. I fhou'd think it a breach of my duty, to fee you plunge yourfelf into fo irretrievable a fate, without acquainting you with my fentiments—if you faw her in the light I do, Sir—you would think on your wedding day with horror.

Mr. H. Why—why—are you mad?

Geo. If you wifhed to keep your engagements a fecret, Sir—I am forry I mention'd the affair, but—

Bel. Oh—'tis no fecret, Sir, I affure you—every body talks of it—for my part, I fhall be quite happy in paying my refpects to my new Aunt—I have put a coral ftring in my tambour already, that I may finifh it time enough for her firft Boy to wear at its chriftening.

Mr. H. Look ye, Sir—I perceive that you have all that backwardnefs in obeying me that I expected, and, in order to conceal it, are attempting to throw the affair into ridicule—but I tell you it will not do—I know what I am about, and my commands fhall not be difputed.

Geo. Commands, Sir!—I am quite at a lofs—

Mr. H. Well then, to prevent further miftakes, I acquaint you, that I defign Lady Dinah for your *Wife*, and not your Mother—and moreover, that the marriage fhall take place in a very few days. [*going.*]—And, d'ye hear?—acquaint your pert Coufin, that the coral ftring will do for your firft Boy.   *Exit* Hargrave.

[*A long paufe, ftaring at each other.*

Bel. So, fo, fo! and is this the end of all the clofetings?

Sir Ch. What the devil!—it muft be all a dream.

Geo. Wife!!—Lady Dinah *my* Wife!

Bel. Ha, ha, ha! dear George, forgive me, but I muft laugh, or I can't exift—ha, ha, ha! oh, my Coufin Dinah!

Geo. Pray, Bella, fpare your mirth, and tell me what I am to do—for I am incapable of thinking.

Bel. Do! why run to Lady Dinah—fling yourfelf at her feet, tell her you had no idea of the blifs that was defigned you—and that you'll make her the tendereft, fondeft Hufband in the world—ha, ha, ha!

Geo. Oh, Coufin, for once forget your fprightlinefs—I cannot bear it—Seymour, what am I to do ?

Sir Ch. My dear George, I pity you from my foul—but I know not what advice to give you.

Bel. Well, then ferioufly I think—ha, ha, ha ! but 'tis impoffible to be ferious——I am aftonifh'd you are not more ftruck with your Father's tender cares for you.

Geo. Have you no mercy, Bella ?

Bel. You have none upon yourfelf, or inftead of ftanding here with that countenance *fi trifle,* you wou'd be with Mr. Drummond.

Geo. He is, indeed, my only refource—I'll fly to him this inftant, and if it fails me—I am the moft miferable man on earth.   [*Exit.*

Sir Cha. What can induce Mr. Hargrave to facrifice fuch a fellow as George, to a Lady Dinah ?——Prepofterous !

Bel. Her rank and fortune—and I dread the lengths to which his obftinacy may carry him ; he has no more refpect for the divinity of Love, than for that of the Ægyptian Apis —Let us find Harriet, and tell her the ftrange ftory ; fhe is not the only perfon, I fear, to whom it will be painful.

Sir Ch. Is it poffible that Lady Dinah, in the depth of her wifdom, can imagine fuch an union proper ?

Bel. Be merciful——Love has forc'd Heroes to forget their valour, and Philofophers their fyftems—no wonder he fhou'd make a Woman forget her wrinkles.   [*Exeunt.*

SCENE, *the Garden.*

Enter JARVIS *and* SUSAN.

Jar. Egad, tis a fervice of danger.

Suf. Danger ! fure you've no qualms ?

Jar. No, no, child—no qualms—the refolution with which I could go thro' an affair of this fort, would in another hemifphere make my fortune—but hang it, in thefe cold northern regions there's no room for a man of genius to ftrike a bold ftroke—the foftering plains of Afia, for fuch talents as mine !

Suf. Now I think England's a very pretty foil.

Jar. Why, aye, if one could be fure of keeping clear of a dozen ill-bred fellows, who decide on the conduct of a man of fpirit at the Old Bailey, then indeed we need not care ; for an air of Ton, and a carriage, on whatever *fprings* it moves, introduces one to the beft circles——But let us confider our bottom——this girl was plac'd under the care of the old gentlewoman, by a perfon of credit.

Suf. Pho, pho, what! she brought a recommendation—don't we know how easily a character is to be had—spotless as silver, or as bright as gold! 'tis a wonder she did not afford a name too; I warrant she had sufficient reasons to conceal her own.

Jar. It does look like it, and there's a mystery in the affair——Now, mysteries, *as my Lady says,* we have a right to explain as we please.

Suf. Aye, to be sure—and this is the explanation. She is an unprotected, artful girl, who having caught a taste for the life of a fine Lady, thinks the shortest way to gratify her longing, is by gaining the heart of some credulous fool, who'll make her his wife for the sake of her—Beauty.

Jar. True——That with this view she told her story to Mr. Drummond, who—innocent soul—not seeing her drift, introduced her here, where she attempts to succeed, by playing off her artillery on the gunpowder constitution of George Hargrave, Esq; the younger.

Suf. Oh, delightful!——why, if I continue with my Lady, I shall be her mistress as long as she lives——and now I think on't, I believe that must be our plan——You and I can be married just the same, you know.

Jar. Oh, just the same, my dear, just the same; nothing shall prevent that—[*aside*] but my being able to coax you out of the Two Hundred.

Suf. Hark! here comes the Justice—slip away, and leave me to manage him—I know I can make him useful——You need not be jealous now.

Jar. Jealous! no, no; I have liv'd among the great too long, to be tormented with so vulgar a passion. [*Ex.* Jar.

Enter JUSTICE.

Juf. Hah, hah! have I caught you, my little Picksey? Come, no struggling——I will have a kiss, by Jingo.

Suf. Lud! you are the strangest Gentleman—[*resisting.*]

Juf. You are wondrous coy, methinks.

Suf. Coy—so I should——What have Gentlewomen without fortune, to recommend 'em else?

Juf. Aye—but that rosy, pouting mouth tells different tales, I warrant, to the fine Gentlemen in London. I have been thinking you'd make a pretty little Housekeeper—yes you would, Hussey—yes you would—will you come and live with me?

Suf. Oh, dear Sir—I should like it vastly; but I think you had better go to London with me——I assure you, my

Lady speaks very highly of your talents in the law——and she has great interest————so, as soon as she is Lady Dinah Hargrave——Your Worship is acquainted with that affair, I suppose.

Jus. Yes, yes; my friend has told me of it—but under strict injunctions of secrecy.

Sus. Secrecy! aye, to be sure——but I dare say Mr. Drummond has been informed of it.

Jus. Oh, I know nothing of *him*—he's queer and close; one can never get him in at a bout——he's not staunch.

Sus. I believe he is not staunch to our match; and if that is prevented, we shall leave the country directly.

Jus. Why, what can prevent it, Sweety?

Sus. Perhaps Mr. Drummond's advice; for *he* can manage Mr. Hargrave.

Jus. Ah——but my advice will go as far as his, I believe; and do you think I'll part with you—you little wicked rogue you? [*chucking her chin.*]

Sus. Then if you find the match is likely to go off, you must use all your interest to bring it to bear; and then we sha'n't part, you little wicked rogue you. [*chucking his chin.*]

Jus. That I will—I'll plead for the wedding as vigorously, as if I had an hundred guineas with a brief.

Sus. Well—but d'ye mind me? I don't like the stranger this same 'Squire usher'd here.

Jus. Not like her! why, she's a devilish fine girl; ——adad, the warm sparkling of her eyes catches one's heart, as if it was made of tinder.

Sus. Upon my word—a devilish fine Girl—the sparkling of her eyes!————

Jus. Oh—I don't mean—that is—Oh, I would rather have one kind look of thine, sweet Mrs. Sukey—for t'other I dare not squint at.

Sus. Hah!—I believe you are a Coquet—but however, I have certain reasons to wish this beautiful Angel out of the house. I have observed looks that I don't like, between her and young Hargrave—and—you comprehend me—whatever interrupts the marriage, we are gone.

Jus. I understand you—you may depend upon me—let me see—how shall we manage to get her out of Drummond's clutches?

Sus. That's your business—I say, that must be done, and you must do it.

Jus. To be sure, Mrs. Susan—let me consider————

H

Suf. We muſt have no qualms, Mr. Juſtice.

Juſ. We will have none---but what your ſmiles, ſweet Sukey, can diſperſe——I muſt venture a little—the tender paſſions make one do any thing. *Omnia vincit amor,* ſay no more.

Suf. She ſhall be ſent packing.

Juſ. Have I not given you the word of a Magiſtrate?—But come now, give me one kiſs, you little dear, cruel, ſoft, ſweet, charming, baggage.

Suf. Oh, fye—you won't aſk for wages, before you've done your work.   *[runs off.*

Juſ. Stop—don't run ſo faſt—don't run ſo faſt, Huſſy— *[following]*   *[Exit.*

SCENE, an *Apartment.*

Enter *Mr.* DRUMMOND *and* GEORGE.

Mr. D. I wiſh I had known it before matters had been carried ſo far——on a ſubject of this nature no woman can be affronted with impunity.

Geo. I am careleſs of her reſentment—I will never be her huſband—nor huſband to any woman, but *her* to whom I have given my vows.

Mr. D. Hah!—have you carried your affair ſo forward?

Geo. Yes, Sir, I have made that enchanting Girl the offer of my heart and hand, and tho' her delicacy forbids her, while our families remain unknown to each other, to give the aſſent my heart aſpires to—yet ſhe allows me to catch hopes, that I would not forfeit to become maſter of the univerſe.

Mr. D. There's a little of the ardor of youth in this— the ardor of youth, George—however, I will not blame you, for twenty years ago, I might have been tempted to enter the liſts with you, myſelf.

Geo. I ſhou'd fear leſs to meet a Hector in the field— in ſuch a cauſe the fury of Achilles would inſpire me—and I would bear off my lovely prize from amidſt the embattled phalanx.

Mr. D. Bravo—I like to ſee a man romantic in his love, and in his friendſhips——the virtues of him who is not an enthuſiaſt in thoſe noble paſſions, will never have ſtrength to riſe into fortitude, patriotiſm, and philanthropy— but here comes your Father, leave us.

Geo. May the ſubject inſpire you with reſiſtleſs eloquence!   *[Exit.*

Enter *Mr.* HARGRAVE.

Mr. D. So, Mr. Hargrave.

Mr. H. So, Mr. Drummond—what, I guefs your bufinefs.

Mr. D. I fuppofe you do, and I hope you are prepared
to hear me with temper.

Mr. H. You'll talk to no purpofe, for I am fixed, and
therefore the temper will fignify nothing.

Mr. D. Strange infatuation! why muft George be
facrificed to your ambition?—furely, it may be gratified
without tying *him* to your Lady Dinah.

Mr. H. How?

Mr. D. By marrying her yourfelf—which, till now,
I fuppofed to have been your defign—and that wou'd have
been fufficiently prepofterous.

Mr. H. What!—make me a fecond time the flave of
hyfterics, longings, and vapours!——no, no, I've got
my neck out of the noofe—catch it there again if you can—
what, her Ladyfhip is not youthful enough for George, I
fuppofe?

Mr. D. True—but a more forcible objection is the dif-
proportion in their minds——it wou'd not be lefs reafon-
able to expect a new element to be produced between earth
and fire, than that felicity fhou'd be the refult of fuch a
marriage.

Mr. H. Pfha, pfha—what, do you fuppofe the whole
world has the fame idle notions about love and conftancy,
and ftuff, that you have? D'ye think, if George was to
become a widower at five and twenty, *he'd* whine all his
life for the lofs of his deary?

Mr. D. Not if his deary, as you call her, fhould be
a Lady Dinah; and if you marry him with no other view
than to procure him a happy widowhood, I admire the
election you have made—but, if fhe fhou'd be like my
loft love—my fainted Harriet—my——oh! Hargrave——

Mr. H. Come, come, I am very forry I have moved
you fo—I did not mean to affect you——come, give me
your hand—'fbud, if a man has any thing to do with one
of you fellows with your fine feelings, he muft be as cautious as if he was carrying a candle in a gunpowder
barrel.

Mr. D. 'Tis over, my friend—but when I can hear
my Harriet named, without giving my heart a fond regret for what I have loft—reproach me—for then, I fhall
deferve it.

Mr. H. Well, well—it fhall be your own way—but
come, let me convince you that you are wrong in this bufinefs
—'fbud! I tell you it has been the ftudy of my life to make
George a great man—I brought Lady Dinah here with no

other defign—and now, when I thought the matter was
brought to bear—when Lady Dinah had confented—and my
Son, as I fuppofed, eager for the wedding——why !—'tis all
a flam !

Mr. D. My good friend—the motives, from which you
wou'd facrifice your Son's happinefs, appear to me fo weak.

Mr. H. Weak!—why, I tell you, I have provided a
wife for George, who will make him, perhaps, one of the
firft men in the kingdom.

Mr. D. That is, fhe would make him a Court Dangler,
an attendant on Minifters levees——one whofe ambition
is to be foftered with the cameleon food of fmiles and nods,
and who would receive a familiar fqueeze with as much
rapture as the plaudits of a nation——oh——fhame—to
transform an independent Englifh Gentleman into fuch a
being !

Mr. H. Well, to cut the argument fhort——the bargain is ftruck, and George fhall marry Lady Dinah, or
never have an acre of my land, that's all.

Mr. D. And he fhall never poffefs a rood of mine, if he
does. [*walking about*]

Mr. H. [*afide*] There, I thought twou'd come to this:
what a fhame it is for a man to be fo obftinate !—but hold—
faith, if fo, I may lofe more than I get by the bargain—
he'll ftick to his word.

Enter JUSTICE.

Juf. I am very much furprized, Mr. Drummond—Sir—
—that I can't be left alone in the difcharge of my magif-
terial duties, but muft be continually thwarted by you.

Mr. D. This interruption, Mr. Juftice, is ill-timed,
and rather out of rule—I cou'd wifh you had chofen another opportunity.

Juf. No opportunity like the prefent—no time like the
prefent, Sir—you've caufe, indeed, to be difpleas'd with
my not obferving rules, when you are continually breaking the laws.

Mr. D. Ha, ha, ha ! let us hear—what hen-rooft robbery
have you to lay to my charge now ?

Juf. Aye, Sir, you may think to turn it off with a joke,
if you pleafe—but for all that, I can prove you to be a
bad member of fociety, for you counteract the wife defigns of our legiflators, and obftruct the operations of juftice—yes, Sir, you do.

Mr. H. Don't be fo warm——what is this affair ?

Juf. Why, the poacher, whom we committed laft night,

Mr. Drummond has releafed, and given money to his family—How can we expect a due obfervance of our laws, when rafcals find encouragement for breaking them?—— Shall Lords and Commons in their wifdom affemble in Parment, to make laws about hares and partridges, only to be laughed at? Oh, 'tis abominable!

Mr. H. Very true; and let me tell you, Mr. Drummond, it is very extraordinary that you will be continually——

Mr. D. Peace, ye men of juftice—I have all the regard to the laws of my country, which it is the duty and intereft of every member of fociety to poffefs——If the man had been a poacher, he fhou'd not have been protected by me——the poor fellow found the hare in his garden, which fhe had confiderably injured.

Mr. H. Ho, ho—what, the rafcal juftifies himfelf! an unqualified man gives reafons for deftroying a hare!— Zounds, if a gang of ruffians fhou'd burn my houfe, wou'd you expect me to hear their reafons?

Juf. Ah, there it works—Sufan's my own [*afide.*]—there can be no reafons—if he had found her in his houfe, in his bed-chamber—in his bed, and offer'd to touch her—I'd profecute him for poaching.

Mr. D. Oh, blufh to avow *fuch* principles!

Mr. H. Look'ee, Mr. Drummond, though you govern George with your whimfical notions, you fha'n't me. —I forefee how it will be as foon as I'm gone—my fences will be cut down—my meadows turned into common—my corn-fields laid open—my woods at the mercy of every man who carries an axe——and, oh—this is noble, this is great!

Mr. D. Indeed, 'tis ridiculous.

Mr. H. I'll take care that my property fha'n't fall a facrifice to fuch whimfies——I'll tye it up, I warrant me— and fo, Juftice, come along. [*going.*]

Mr. D. We were talking on a fubject, Mr. Hargrave, of more importance, at prefent, than this; and, I beg you'll hear me farther.

Mr. H. Enough has been faid already, Mr. Drummond, —or if not, I'll give you one anfwer for all——I fhall never think myfelf obliged to ftudy the humour of a man, who thinks in fuch oppofition to me; I have a humour of my own, which I am determined to gratify, in feeing George a great man—He fhall marry Lady Dinah in two days; and all the fine reafoning in the world, you will fee, has lefs ftrength than my refolution—'Sbud, if I can't have the willing obedience of a Son, I'll enjoy the prerogatives of a Father———Come along, Juftice.   [*Exit.*

Juf. D'ye hear with what a fine *firm* tone he fpeaks ?—This was only a political ftroke, to reftore the balance of power.

Mr. D. Why don't you follow, Sir? [*Exit* Juftice.] My fon fhall be a great Man !—To fuch a vanity as this, how many have been facrificed !—He fhall be great—The happinefs of love, the felicities that flow from a fuitable union, his heart fhall be a ftranger to—but he fhall convey *my name,* deck'd with titles, to pofterity, though, to purchafe thefe diftinctions, he lives a wretch—This is the filent language of the heart, which we hold up to ourfelves as the voice of Reafon and Prudence.

Enter EMILY.

Mifs Morley !—Why this penfive air ?

Em. I am a little diftrefs'd, Sir—the delicacy of the motive which induced you to place me here, I am perfectly fenfible of—yet———

Mr. D. Yet—what, my dear Child ?

Em. Do not think me capricious, if I intreat you to take me back to your own houfe, till my uncle arrives—I cannot think of remaining here.

Mr. D. Then 'tis as I hoped [*afide.*]—What can have difgufted you ?—Come, be frank ; confider me as a friend, to whom you may fafely open your heart.

Em. Your goodnefs, Sir, is exceffive—Shall I confefs—the Lady who will foon have moft right here, treats me unkindly.

Mr. D. That you can't wonder at—Be affured, I will effectually defend you from her infults———But do you not pity poor George, for the fate his father defigns him ?

Em. Yes—I do pity him.

Mr. D. If I dared, I would go ftill further—I would hope, that, as his happinefs depends on you—

Em. Sir !

Mr. D. Let me not alarm you—I am acquainted with his paffion, and wifh to know that 'tis not difpleafing to you.

Em. So circumftanced, Sir—what can I fay ?—He is deftined to be the hufband of another.

Mr. D. It is enough—I bind myfelf to you from this moment, and promife to effect your happinefs, if within the compafs of my abilities or fortune. But, that I may know my tafk—favour me with the key to your Uncle's character.

Em. My Uncle poffeffes a heart, Sir, that would do him honour, if he would be guided by it—but unhappily he has conceived an opinion that his temper is too flexible—that he is too eafily perfuaded—and the confequence is—he'll never be perfuaded at all.

Mr. D. I am forry to hear that—a man who is obftinate from *fuch* a miftake, muft be in the moft incurable ftage of the diforder. However, we'll attack this man of might—his flexibility fhall be befieged, and if it won't capitulate, we'll undermine it.

Em. Ah, Sir! my Uncle is in a ftate of mind ill prepared for yielding—He returned from Spain with eager pleafure to his native country; but the difguft he has conceiv'd for the alteration of manners during his abfence, has given him an impatience that you will hardly be able to combat.

Mr. D. Take courage—let me now lead you back to your young companions—I am obliged to be abfent a fhort time—but I'll watch over you, and, if poffible, lead you to happinefs. [*Exit Drummond leading Emily.*

Enter JUSTICE. [*tipfy*]

Juf. • Where the devil does my clerk ftay with Burn!
• But I know I'm right—yes, yes, 'tis a clear cafe. By the
• ftatute *Anno Primo Caroli Secundum*—obtaining goods on
•• falfe pretences, felony, with benefit—hum—with benefit.
• —Now obtaining entrance into houfes, upon falfe preten-
• ces, muft be worfe—I have no doubt but it amounts to a
• burglary, and that I fhall be authorized to commit——Ho!
• here they are! where is my clerk and Burn? [*Exit.*

Enter Mr. HARGRAVE *and Lady* DINAH.

Mr. H. Aye, aye, here's a pretty bufinefs—bringing this Girl into my houfe now is the confequence of Mr. Drummond's fine feelings—he will never take my advice—but I'll fhew him who is beft qualified to fift into an affair of this fort—and yet *I am* a little puzzled—a ftroller—

Lady. D. It is, doubtlefs, a ftrange ftory, Mr. Hargrave —and I beg that you will yourfelf queftion my fervant concerning it.

Mr. H. Why, what can fhe mean—what can her defign be?

Lady D. To *you* I fhou'd imagine her defign muft be very obvious, 'though Mr. Drummond's penetration was fo eafily eluded——By affuming the airs and manners of a perfon of rank, fhe doubtlefs expects to impofe on the credulity of fome young heir, and to procure——a jaunt to Scotland——*that,* Mr. Hargrave, I take to be her defign.

Mr. H. Hoh, ho, is it fo——now I underſtand your Ladyſhip—if your man can prove what he aſſerts, be aſſured, Madam, ſhe ſhall not ſtay in my houſe another moment—I'll young heir the baggage.

Lady D. But conſider, dear Mr. Hargrave, before you take any ſteps in this affair——that 'tis poſſible, we may have been deceived, for tho' my ſervant avows having been on the moſt intimate terms with her, he may be miſtaken in her perſon, you know.

Har. Oh, Madam, I ſhall inquire into that—ſhe ſhall pick up no young heirs here, I warrant her—I ſhall ſee into that immediately.   [*Going.*

Enter Juſtice, *leading in* JARVIS *by the button.*

Juſt. Here's the young man—the witneſs—I have brought him up in order to his examination.——Here,—do you ſtand there.—In the firſt place,—[*ſettling his wig*] in the firſt place, how old are you ?

Har. Fiddle de de——What ſignifies how old he is ?

Juſt. Why, yes it does—for—if he is not of age——

Har. Pſha, pſha—I'll examine him myſelf. How long is it ſince you left the ſtrollers you were engaged with ?

Jar. It is about two years ſince I had the honour of being taken into my Lady's ſervice,—and at that time I left the company.

Har. And did you leave the young woman in the company at that time ?

Jar. I did, Sir, and I have never ſeen her ſince till now.

Har. I am ſtrangely puzzled——I don't know what to think——

Juſt. It is indeed a difficult caſe—a very difficult caſe—— I remember Burn in the chapter on Vagrants——

Har. Prithee, be ſilent—at this time you are not likely to clear up matters at all.

Juſt. A Juſtice be ſilent !—a ſilent Juſtice !— a pretty thing indeed—are we not the very mouth of the law ?

Har. What does your Ladyſhip adviſe ?

Lady D. I adviſe !—I don't adviſe, Mr. Hargrave.

Juſt. Why then, let the parties be confronted—

Har. Aye—let the parties be confronted.

Jar. Ay, ay, let us be confronted: if I once ſpeak to her, ſhe'll be too much daſh'd to be able to deny the charge.

Enter Servant.

Ser. Did your honour call ?

Har. Go and tell my daughter, that I deſire ſhe'll bring her viſitant here—the young Lady.

Jar. [*Afide*] Two glaffes of brandy, and tremble yet !—
.I wifh I had fwallow'd the third bumper.

La-ly D. Now, Mr. Hargrave, it will be exceedingly im-
, proper, that I fhould be prefent at this interview, fo I fhall
retire till the affair is fettled,   [*Going.*

. *Mr. H.* 'Sbud, my Lady, if you go, I'll go too—and the
·, Juftice may fettle it as well as he can.

Juf. Nay, if you are for that—I fhall be gone in a crack
, —I won't be left in the lurch—not I.

, *Lady D.* Blefs me! I am furprifed—only confider what an
imputation may be thrown on my character.

Enter HARRIET *and* EMILY.

So—now 'tis determin'd.

Har. Robert inform'd us, Sir, that you requefted our at-
·tendance.

Mr. H. Yes, Harriet—I did fend Robert—'tis about an
odd affair—I had rather—but I don't know—pray, Madam—
.[*to Emily*] be fo kind to tell us if you know any thing of
that perfon—[*pointing to* Jarvis.]

Em. No, Sir, I believe not—I do not recollect—I may
·have feen him before.

. *Jar.* Oh, Mifs Jenny—you don't recollect—what, you
.have forgot your old companion William Jarvis ?

Em. I do not remember indeed, that I was ever honour'd
·with fuch a companion——and the miftake you have made of
my name, convinces me that I never was.

. *Jar.* Piha, pfha—this won't do *now*—you was always a
good actrefs, but behind the fcenes, you know, we ufed to
·come down from our ftilts, and talk in our own proper perfons
—Why fure, you will not pretend to forget our adventures at
Colchefter—the affair of the Blue Domino at Warwick——
nor the plot which you and Mrs. Varnifh laid againft the
Manager at Beconsfield.

. *Har.* Dear Sir, nothing is fo evident, as that the man
has miftaken this Lady for another perfon—I—hope you'll
permit us to go without hearing any more of his impertinence.

: *Mr. H.* If he is miftaken, no excufes will be fufficient—I
don't know what to fay——'tis a perplexing bufinefs—but I
wifh you wou'd be fo kind to anfwer the man, Madam.

, *Em.* Aftonifhment has kept me filent till now, Sir—and I
muft ftill be filent——for I have not yet been taught to make
defences.

I

Enter GEORGE *behind* JARVIS.

Jar. Dear Madam—why surely you have not forgot how often you have been my Juliet, and I your Alexander.

Geo. Hark you, Sir,——if you dare utter another word to that Lady, I'll break every bone in your body—leave the room, rafcal, this inftant.

Mr. H. You are too hot, George—he fhall ftay—and fince things have gone fo far, I'll fift the ftory to the bottom—If the young Gentlewoman is not what he reprefents her, fhe has nothing to fear—Speak boldly——where did you laft fee that Lady?

Juf. Aye, fpeak boldly——give her a few more circum-ftances, perhaps fome of them may hit—People on occafions of this fort have generally fhort memories.

Geo. Surely, Sir, you cannot allow thefe horrid—

Mr. H. I do allow, Sir—and if you can't be filent, leave the room.

Juf. Yes, Sir, or elfe you'll be committed for contempt of Court. Now, for your name, child, your name, and that of your family.

Em. The name of my family, demanded on fuch an oc-cafion, I think myfelf bound to conceal—my filence on that fubject, hitherto arofe from a point of delicacy—that motive is now greatly ftrengthened, and I refufe to difcover a name —which my imprudent conduct has difgraced.

Juf. Ho, ho—pray let the Lady be treated with refpect—a perfon of Confequence—ftands upon Conftitutional ground ——a Patriot, I'll affure you——fhe refufes to anfwer Inter-rogatories.

Geo. Sir, I cannot be any longer a filent witnefs of thefe in-fults—Your prefence, Madam, fupports that rafcal, or he fhou'd feel the immediate effect of my refentment.

Lady D. Your refentment will be unneceffary Sir, if he is not fupported by truth——I fhall take care that he is properly punifh'd. [*Enter Servant.*

Sir. A Gentleman in a coach-and-fix enquires for your honour—his name is Morley.

Em. Hah—'tis my Uncle—I no longer dread his prefence —now, Sir, you will be fatisfied concerning my family.
[*Exeunt Emily and Harriet.*

Mr. H. [*to Lady D.*] Her Uncle—Heavens! Madam, what have we done! [*Exit Hargrave.*

Lady D. Done!—nothing—madnefs! [*afide.*

Juf. So, fo——the niece of a man who keeps a coach and ſix !——we are got into a wrong box here—— ſhe can be no Patriot, our Patriots don't ride in coaches and ſix.

Geo. Stay, Sir——we have not done with you yet——you muſt now exhibit another part in this ſcene—what ſays your oracle Burn to ſuch a fellow as this, Juſtice?

Juf. Ay, you raſcal —— 'tis now your turn—thou art a vilifier, a cheat, an impoſtor— 'tis a downright conſpiracy— The niece of a man who keeps a coach and ſix !—why, how doſt think to eſcape? thou'lt cut a noble figure in the pillory, Mr. " Alexander the Great."

Jar. Sir,—your honours—I humbly crave pardon for my miſtake—I cou'd have ſworn the Lady had been my old acquaintance, the likeneſs is ſo ſtrong.—But I humbly aſk pardon——my Lady !——

Lady D. Expect no protection from me, I diſcharge you from my ſervice from this moment.——The dilemma into which you have deceived me excites my warmeſt reſentment.

Geo. Since Your Ladyſhip gives him up, he has no other protection—Who's there? [*Enter Servants*] Secure this fellow till I have leiſure to inquire into the bottom of the affair—*he is only the Agent,* I am convinced.

Jar. [*Aſide.*] Aye, Sir, but I am dumb—or we ſhall loſe the reward.] I beſeech your honour— 'twas all a miſtake.

Geo. Take him away. [*Exeunt ſervants with Jarvis.*

Lady D, [*Aſide.*] Hah—are you ſuſpicious, Sir?—I hope Suſan has not put me in this fellow's power—I muſt be ſure of that. [*Exit.*

Juf. 'Tis a conſpiracy, that's certain—and will, I believe, come under *Scan. Mag.* for 'tis a moſt ſcandalous Libel—but hold——'gad-ſo——let me ſee——it can be no libel; 'tis a falſe ſtory——if it had been true——aye, then indeed——if it had been true——but I'll go home and conſult Burn, and you ſhall know what he ſays, Egad, it won't be amiſs to get out of this Morley's way, [*Aſide.* [*Exit Juſtice.*

Geo. Surely ſhe muſt have been privy to this ſcandalous plot—but 'tis no matter—my fate is at its criſis.—Mr. Morley's arrival fixes it.——At this moment my fortitude forſakes me, and I tremble to meet the Man, on whoſe caprice depends, the value of my exiſtence.

END OF THE FOURTH ACT.

A C T   V.

SCENE, *an Apartment.*

Enter Mr. MORLEY *and* EMILY.

MORLEY.

A Pretty freak indeed!—a pretty freak, in return for the care and folicitude with which I have watch'd over you——I have broke with the Doctor for his fhare in this romantic affair.

Em. I am much concerned, Sir, that compaffion to my fituation fhould have led that worthy Man to take any ftep that you can think unpardonable——but when he found he cou'd not move my refolution, he thought it his duty to accommodate me with a retreat amongft perfons of reputation.

Mor Retreat!——fo, whilft I was condemning my fweet innocent Niece for ftubbornnefs, wilfulnefs, and ingratitude—fhe was only gone to a *retreat* to fit under elms, liften to the cawing of rooks, and carve her melancholy ftory on the young bark—Oh, Emily, Emily! you ought to be made repent of this retreat, as you call it, as long as you live.

Em. Indeed, Sir, I do repent.

Mor. What's that?—repent!—my dear Emily, I am rejoiced to hear you fay fo—I knew you was always a good Girl on the, whole——come, it fha'n't be a misfortune to you——I'll make Baldwin fwear, before the ceremony, that he'll never reproach—

Em. Sir, I muft not deceive you——my repentance does not concern Mr. Baldwin—he is—pardon me, Sir——my fentiments with regard to him, are, if poffible, ftrengthen'd.

Mor. Are they fo, Miftrefs? then farewell to humourings—fince your fentiments are fo ftrong, your refolution cannot be weak——'twill enable you to bear this dreaded fate with heroifm.

Em. I am glad you can be fo fportive with my unhappinefs, Sir——where you jeft with mifery, you always defign to leffen it.

Mor. Aye, that won't do —— the eafinefs of my temper, Girl, has been my great misfortune. I never made a miftake in trade in my life, never, but have been *perfuaded*, and liften'd to *advice*, till I have been half ruined——but I'll be refolute now for your fake.

Em. Surely, Sir——

Mor. Aye, aye—I underſtand that ſpeaking face—there is not a line in it, but calls me Monſter—however, Madam, after your retreat, you can never expect to be the wife of another—ſo ſnap Baldwin while you can.

Em. Oh, Sir, allow me to live ſingle, I have no wiſh for the married ſtate—ſince he to whom my heart is devoted muſt be the huſband of another.

Mor. No wiſh for the married ſtate! ha, ha, ha!——why, 'tis the ultimate wiſh of every woman's heart—you all want Huſbands, from your doll to your ſpectacles.

Em. The perſon with whom one enters into ſo important an union ſhou'd be at leaſt agreeable, or——.

Mor. What an age this is!—Why, huſſey, in the days of your great Grand-mother, a Girl on the point of marriage had never dared to look above her lover's beard—and would have been a wife a week before ſhe cou'd have told the colour of her huſband's eyes—But, now, a Girl of eighteen will ſtare her ſuitor confidently in the face, and, after five minutes converſation, give an account of every feature and peculiarity, from his brow to his buckle—But pray, Madam, what is it in Baldwin now, that ſo particularly hits your fancy?

Em. His perſon is ungraceful, his manner aſſuming, and his mind effeminate.

Mor. Very true—and is not this the deſcription of all the young men of the age?—but he has five thouſand a year, that's not quite ſo common a circumſtance. Come, take the pencil again, lay on coarſer colours, or you won't convince me the picture's a bad one—conſidering the times.

Em. Hah!—how different is Mr. Hargrave!—if I could urge his merit [*aſide*]——You have heard my objections ſo often, Sir, that the repetition can have no weight——but, ſurely, I may urge my happineſs.

Mor. By all means, it ſhall be conſider'd, therefore—John, order my carriage up, we are going directly—tho' you don't deſerve it—the very moment we reach Groſvenor-ſtreet, you ſhall be tied faſt to Baldwin, who is now waiting there with the parſon at his elbow—and we'll this moment ſtep into the carriage, and away as briſkly, as if Cupid was our coachman——come now, don't put on that melancholy air—'tis only to turn the tables—fancy that I hate Baldwin—that you are driving to Scotland, and I purſuing you—why the horſes will move ſo ſlowly, you'll be ready to ſwear they don't gallop above three rood an hour.

Em. I entreat you, dear Sir, ſtay, at leaſt, till to-morrow.——Oh, where is Mr. Drummond? [*aſide.*

Mor. Not a moment.

Em. You have not yet feen Mr. Drummond, to whom I am fo much oblig'd.

Mor. I have made enquiries, and have heard a very extraordinary character of Mr. Drummond ; we can make him acknowledgments by letter—and you may fend him gloves.—— I know your defign, you hope he will be able to talk me out of my refolution—and, perhaps, I may be a little afraid of it myfelf,—and fo, to avoid that danger, we'll go directly.

Em. 'Tis fo late, Sir,—and the night is dark.——[*Afide*] Yet why fhould I wifh to ftay here ?

Mor. No more trifling—conduct me to the family, that we may take leave. If you complain of this as an act of tyranny—be comforted, Child, 'tis the laft you'll experience from me—my authority will expire with the night, and to-morrow morning, I fhall be my dear Niece Baldwin's moft humble fervant.   *Exeunt.*

Enter GEORGE *and Sir* CHARLES.

Geo. What, refufe me your affiftance in fuch an hour—talk to me of prudence in a moment when I muft be mad, if I am human ! yes, be prudent, Sir, be prudent,—the man who can be difcreet when his friend's happinefs is at ftake, may gain the approbation of his own heart, but mine renounces him——Where can Mr. Drummond be ?

Sir Ch. I am at your command in every thing——I afk you only to reflect.

Geo. Yes, I do reflect, that in a few hours fhe will be irrecoverably another's—loft to me for ever—unfeeling brute ! to facrifice fuch a Woman to a man whom fhe defpifes !

Sir Ch. What then is your refolution ?

Geo. There is but one way—fhe hangs on the point of a precipice, from which, if I do not fnatch her in an inftant, nothing can retrieve her.—We will follow the carriage on horfeback ; let your chaife attend us with our fervants—I'll force her from this tyrant Uncle, carry her inftantly to Dover, and in a few hours, breathe out my foul at her feet—in fweet fecurity in France.

Sir Ch. Confidering your plan is an *impromptu*, I admire its confiftency—but, my dear George, have you weighed all its confequences ?——your Father——

Geo. Will perhaps difinherit me—be it fo—I have fix hundred a year independent of his will—and fix hundred a year in France with Emily Morly—kingdoms ! empires ! paradife !

' *Sir Ch.* But are you certain she will partake it with you?

' *Geo.* No——but suppofing the worft—I fhall, at leaft,
' have had the happinefs to preferve her from a fate fhe dreads
' —for the reft I will truft to time and my ardent paffion.

' *Sir Ch.* Pity the days of chivalry are over, or what ap-
' plaufe might'ft thou not expect——advent'rous Knight!

' *Geo.* Come, we have not a moment to lofe—let us get
' our people ready to follow, the inftant the carriage fets out.

Sir Ch. But, George—George—I'll not accompany you a
ftep, after the Lady's in your protection—for if your Father
fhou'd furmife that I have any hand in the *enlevement*, I can
hope for no fuccefs, when I afk him for my charming Harriet.

Geo. Agreed—let me have your chaife, and leave me to my
fortune—I will not endanger your happinefs—this key will let
you in at the garden-door—you may give fifty reafons for
your fhort abfence.——Now, Cupid, Venus, Jove and
Juno, leap into your chariots, and defcend to our affiftance.

[*Exeunt Sir* Charles *and* George.
Enter Lady DINAH.

Lady D. She's gone, and my alarms are at an end—'tis
plain I had never the leaft foundation for my fears—what
pafs'd in the garden was mere gallantry, and the effects of her
art; he fuffered her Uncle to carry her off with an indifference
that tranfports me. How weak have I been, to allow my credulity to be impofed on by their fuggeftions, and my temper
ruffled at a time when 'twas of fo much importance to me to
have been ferene!

Enter SUSAN.

Sufan. Oh, my Lady, fhe's gone—the delightful obftinacy of the old Uncle—It is well Mr. Drummond was not
here—I was afraid——

Lady D. Your joy wears a very familiar afpect—I know
fhe's gone.

Sufan. I beg pardon, my Lady—I thought I might con-
gratulate your Ladyfhip on her being carried off—I was terri-
bly afraid——

Lady D. Yes, you have had moft extraordinary fears on
the occafion. You ought to have known, that the man
whom I had receiv'd as my Lover, could never have felt any
thing like a ferious paffion for fuch a girl as that.

Suf. So, fo, fo! how foon our fpirits are got up! [*afide.*]
I am fure, my Lady, 'twas not I who occafioned the interview in the garden to-day, that fo enraged you, and con-
firmed your fears——you was ready enough then to believe
all that was faid againft her.

Lady D. How dare you reproach me with the errors which you led me into ?—'twas your fears I was govern'd by, and not my own ; and your ridiculous plot was as abfurd as your fears.

Suf. As to the plot, my Lady, I am fure 'twas a good one, and would have fent her packing, if the Uncle hadn't come——'twasn't our fault he came——We have had the fame trouble, and—fervice is no inheritance, and I hope your Ladyfhip will confider——

Lady D. How dare you think of a reward for fuch conduct ? —If you obtain my pardon, you ought to be highly gratified —leave me, Infolent, this moment.

Suf. [*muttering.*] Ha !—and dare you ufe me in this manner ?——I am glad you have betrayed yourfelf in time, when I can take a fevere revenge ? [*afide.*]   [*Ex.* Suf.

Lady D. I have gone too far——Now muft I court my fervant, to forget the refentment which her impertinence occafioned——Well, 'tis but for a fhort time——the marriage over, and I have done with her— 'I muft retire to my apart-' ment, to recover my compofure : perhaps he'll vifit me there ' —but not to talk of veneration and refpect again—Oh ! I'll ' torment him for that.   Nothing gives a Woman fo fine an ' opportunity of plaguing her Lover, as an affectation off jea-' loufy : if fhe feels it, fhe's his Slave ; but, whilft fhe affects ' it—his Tyrant·   [*Exit.*

Enter BELLA *and* HARRIET.

Har. How very unfortunate, that Mr. Drummond is abfent !—he would have oppofed the reafoning of Lady Dinab, and prevented their departure——Sure, never any thing was fo cruel.

Bel. Oh, there's no bearing it——Your Father is quite a manageable being, compared to this odd, provoking mortal, whofe imagined flexibility baffles art, reafon, and every thing.

Har. Never fhall I forget the look, wild, yet compofed— agonized tho' calm, which fhe gave me, as her Uncle led her out.   Her Lover muft poffefs ftrange fentiments, to refolve to marry her, in fpite of her averfion.

Bel. Sentiments ! my dear—why he's a modern fine Gentleman ; there is nothing he's fo much afraid of as a fond Wife —If I was Mifs Morley, I'd affect a moft formidable fondnefs, and ten to one but fhe'd get rid of him.

Har. I wonder where Sir Charles is—he pafs'd me in the hall, and faid in a hafty manner, he muft tear himfelf from me for half an hour.

Bel. I wonder rather where your Brother is——but the heart of a woman in love, is as unnatural as the oftrich's ; it is no longer alive to any fentiment but one, and the tendereſt connexions are abforbed in its paſſion.

Har. I hope it is not in your own heart, you find this picture of love.

Enter Sir CHARLES.

Bel. Oh—here's one of our truants, but where's the other ?—poor George, I fuppoſe, is binding his brow with willows.

Sir Ch. That's not George's ſtyle in love—he has too much ſpirit to croſs his arms, and talk to his ſhadow, when he may employ his hours to more advantage at the feet of a fair Lady.

Bel. What do you mean ?

Har. Where is my Brother ?

Sir Ch. On the road to France.

Both. France !

Sir Ch. Unleſs Mr. Morley has as much valour as obſtinacy—for George has purfued him, and, by this time, I dare fwear has gained poffeffion of his Niece.

Bel. Oh! how I doat on his Knight-errantry !—commend me to a lover, who, inſtead of patiently fubmitting to the circumſtances that feparate him from the object of his paſſion,—boldly takes the reins of Fortune in his own hands, and *governs* the accidents which he can't avoid.

Har. How can you praiſe ſuch a daring conduct ? I tremble for the confequences !

Sir Ch. What confequences, Madam, can he dread, who fnatches the woman he loves from the arms of the man ſhe hates ?

Enter Servant.

Ser. My Maſter, Sir, is returned—the Lady fainted in the chaiſe, and he has carried her to Mr. Drummond's.

Ch. The devil !—is he at home ?

Ser. No, Sir—and Mr. Morley is come back too—he drove thro' the gates this minute.

Bel. Nay, then George will loſe her at laſt—he was a fool for not purfuing his route.

Sir Ch. He has no chance now, but thro' Mr. Drummond ; and what can he hope ? Mr. Drummond has only reaſon on his ſide, and the paſſions of three to combat.

Bel. Ay, here he comes—and Mr. Hargrave, as loud as his huntſman.

Har. Let us fly to the parlour, and then we can fend intelligence of what paſſes to George. *[Exeunt.*

K

Enter Mr. MORLEY *and Mr.* HARGRAVE.

Mr. M. Yes, yes, 'tis fact—matter of fact, upon my honour—Your Son was the perfon who took her out of the coach.

Mr. H. Sir, it is impoffible!—ha, ha, ha!—my Son!—why, he's under engagements that wou'd make it madnefs.

Mr. M. Then, Sir, you may depend upon it, the fit is on him now, for he clapt Emily into a chaife, whilft an impudent puppy faften'd on me——egad! twenty years ago I'd have given him fauce to his Cornifh hug—I could not difcern his face—but t'other I'll fwear to.

Mr. H. George! look for George there! I'll convince you, Sir, inftantly——ha, ha!

Enter HARRIET.

Mr. H. Where's George?

Har. Sir, my Brother is at Mr. Drummond's.

Mr. H. There! I knew it could not be him, though you would not be perfuaded.

Mr. M. What a plague! you can't perfuade me out of my fenfes—Your Son, I aver, took her out of the coach—with her own confent, no doubt, and on an honourable defign, without doubt—Sir, I give you joy of your daughter.

Mr. H. If it is on an honourable defign, they may live on their honour, or ftarve with it——not a fingle fous fhall they have of me—but I won't yet believe my George cou'd be fuch a fool.

Mr. M. Fool! Sir——The man who loves Emily gives no fuch proof of folly neither——but fhe fhall be punifhed for hers——'twas a concerted affair, I fee it plainly, all agreed upon—but fhe fhall repent.

Mr. H. Your refentment, Sir, is extraordinary—I muft tell you that my Son's anceftry, or the eftate to which he is heir—if he has not forfeited by his difobedience, are not objects for the contempt of any man.

Mr. M. Very likely, Sir,—but they are objects to which I fhall never be reconciled——What! have I been toiling thefe thirty years in Spain, to make my Niece a match for any man in England—to have her fortune fettled by an adventure in a poft-chaife, an evening's frolick for a young fpark, who had nothing to do but pufh the old fellow into a corner, and whifk off with the girl? Sir, if there was not another man in the kingdom, your Son fhou'd not have my confent to marry Emily.

Mr. H. And if there was not another woman in England, I'd fuffer the name of Hargrave to be annihilated, rather than he fhould be hufband to your Niece. [*Hargrave and Morley walk about the Stage difordered.*]

Enter Mr. DRUMMOND.

Mr. D. Gone!—her Uncle arrived, and the amiable girl gone----What infatuation, Mr. Hargrave, cou'd render you fo blind to the happinefs that awaited your family?——I'll follow this obdurate man—where's George?—look for George there—he fhall hear reafon.

Mr. H. There, Sir——that's the perfon to whom you muft addrefs your complaints.

Mr. D. Unfortunate!—I have made difcoveries, that muft have fhaken even your prejudices—[*to Mr. Hargrave*]—but this Uncle!—furely, my dear Harriet, you might have prevailed.

Har. Sir, this gentleman is Mr. Morley——Mr. Drummond, Sir.

Mr. D. Hah! I beg pardon, Sir, I am rejoiced to fee you; I underftood you were gone.

Mr. M. I was gone, Sir; but I was robb'd of my Niece on the road—fhe was taken out of my coach, and carried off—which forced me to return.

Mr. D. Carried off!

Mr. H. Aye, Sir, carried off by George, whom you have trained to fuch a knowledge of his duty.

Mr. M. Stopt on the King's highway, Sir, by the fiery youth, and my Niece dragg'd from my fide.

Mr. D. Admirable!

Mr. H. What's this right too?—By heaven, it is not to be borne.

Mr. D. Where are they?

Har. At your houfe, Sir——

Mr. M. What a country am I fallen into! can a perfon of your age and character approve of fo rafh and daring——

Mr. H. Let George do what he will—he's fure of his approbation.

Mr. D. Gentlemen—if you are fure Mifs Morley is at my houfe, I am patience itfelf—fhe is too rich a prize to be gained without fome warfare.

Mr. M. Sir, I am refolved to——

Enter Lady DINAH.

[*Exit* HARRIET *frighten'd*].

Lady D. So, Mr. Hargrave! fo, Sir!—what, your Son—this new infult deprives me of utterance—but your Son—what is the reafon of this complicated outrage?

Mr. H. My dear Lady Dinah, I am as much enraged as you can be—but he fhall fulfill his engagements—depend on it, he fhall.

Mr. M. Engagements!—what the young Gentleman was engaged too!—a very fine youth! upon my word.

Lady D. [*to Mr. Hargrave*] Your honour is concern'd, Sir—and if I was fure he was drawn in by the girl's art, and that he was convinced of the impropriety———

Mr. M. Drawn in by the girl's art!—whatever caufe I may have to be offended with my Niece's conduct, Madam, no perfon fhall fpeak of her with contempt in my prefence— I prefume, this gentleman's fon was engaged to your daughter, but that's not a fufficient reafon for———

Lady D. Daughter! impertinent!——No, Sir, 'twas to *me* that he was engaged—and, but for the arts of your Niece———

Mr. M. To you!——A matrimonial negociation between that young Fellow and you!——Nay then, 'fore George, I don't wonder at your ill temper———A difappointment in love at *your* time of life muft be the devil.

Lady D. Mr. Hargrave, do you fuffer me to be thus infulted?

Mr. H. Why, my Lady, we muft bear fomething from this Gentleman——the miftake we made about his Niece, was a very ugly bufinefs.

Mr. D. I entreat you, Madam, to retire from a Family, to whom, if you fuffer me to explain myfelf———

Lady D. What new infolence is this?

Mr. D. I would fpare you, my Lady, but you will not fpare yourfelf——Blufh then, whilft I accufe you of entering into a bafe league with your Servants, to blaft the reputation of an amiable young Lady, and drive her from the protection of Mr. Hargrave's family.

Mr. H. What! a league with her Servants? [*afide.*]

Lady D. And how dare you accufe me of this——Am I to anfwer for the conduct of my fervants?

Mr. D. The *villainy* of your fervants is the confequence of thofe principles with which you have poifon'd their minds. Robb'd of their religion, they were left without fupport—againft temptations to which *you*, Madam, have felt, Philofophy oppofes its fhield in vain.

Lady D. · I feel his fuperiority to my inmoft foul—but
· he fhall not fee his triumph [*afide.*] —Is it your virtue
· which prompts you to load me with injuries, to induce Mr.
· Hargrave to break through every tie of honour—through
· the moft facred engagements!

Mr. D. · I have juft heard thefe terms, nearly as much
· proftituted by your fervants, who reproach you with not
· keeping your engagements to them.

Lady D. Ha! Am I then betrayed ? [*aside.*]

Enter GEORGE, *leading* EMILY.

Geo. Mifs Morley, Sir, commanded me to lead her to you—I cannot afk you to pardon a rafhnefs, of which I do not repent.

Mr. H. Then I fhall *make* you, I fancy.

Mr. M. Hah—did you really wifh to return to me ?

Em. I left Mr. Drummond's, Sir, the moment I knew you were here.

Mr. M. That's a good girl—I'll remember it. Come, child, the coach is at the door, and we muft make fpeed to retrieve our loft time. But have a care, young Gentleman, —tho' I have pardon'd your extravagance once, a fecond attempt fhall find me prepared for your reception.

Geo. If Mifs Morley confents to go with you, Sir, you have no fecond attempt to fear. But fince this moment is the crifis of our fate, thus I entreat you [*kneeling*]—you, to whom I have fworn eternal love, to become my wife. Confent, my charming Emily, and every moment of my future life fhall thank you.

Mr. M. So, fo, fo !

Mr. H. What, without my leave ? } [*All together.*]

Lady D. Amazing !

Em. At fuch a moment as this, meanly to difguife my fentiments would be unworthy of the woman, to whom you offer fuch a facrifice— obtain the confent of thofe who have a right to difpofe of us, and I'll give you my hand at the altar.

Mr. M. That you will not, my frank Madam—fo no more ceremony, but away. [*feizing her arm, and going off.*]

Mr. D. And will you go, impenetrable man—I have difcovered, Sir, that your Niece is the daughter of Major Morley, who was one of the earlieft friends of my youth— He would not have borne the diftrefs fhe now endures—— I will be a father to his orphan Emily, and enfure the felicity of two children, on the point of being facrificed to the ambition and avarice of thofe, on whofe hearts Nature has graven duties, which they wilfully mifpel.

Lady D. What, Sir, are you not content with the infults you have offer'd to me and Mr. Hargrave, but you muft interfere with this Gentleman in the difpofal of his Niece !

Mr. M. What right have you, Sir, to difpofe of our Children ?

Mr. H. Aye, very true, you don't know how to value the authority of a parent.

Drum. Miſtaken Men! into what an abyſs of miſery——perhaps of guilt, wou'd you plunge them!—they claim from you happineſs, and you with-hold it—they ſhall receive it from me. I will ſettle the jointur'd land of my Harriet on Miſs Morley, and George ſhall *now* partake that fortune to which I have already made him heir.

Mr. H. Ay, there's no ſtopping him—what can theſe ſervants have told him, that makes him ſo warm?—Egad, I'll hear their tale.   [*Exit, unperceived by Lady Dinah.*

Mr. M. Why, Sir, this is extraordinary friendſhip indeed! ſettle jointur'd lands—I am glad Brother Tom had prudence enough to form ſuch a connection, 'twas ſeldom he minded the main chance—Honour and a greaſy knapſack, running about after ragged colours, inſtead——

Mr. D. Sir, *I* have ſerved, and I love the profeſſion.—— The army is not more the ſchool of honour than of philoſophy —A true ſoldier is a citizen of the world; he conſiders every man of honour as his brother, and the urbanity of his heart gains his Country *ſubjects,* whilſt his ſword only vanquiſhes her *foes.*

Mr. M. Nay, if you have all this Romance, I don't wonder at your propoſal—however, tho' your jointure lands might have been neceſſary for Major Morly's Daughter—My Niece, Sir, if ſhe marries with my conſent, ſhall be obliged to no man for a fortune.

Lady D. The inſolence of making me witneſs to this is inſupportable—Is this you, Sir, who this very morning paid your vows to me?

Geo. Pardon, Madam, the error of this morning; I imagined myſelf paying my devoirs to a Lady who was to become my Mother.

Lady D. Your Mother! Sir——Your Mother!——Mr. Hargrave——ha, where is Mr. Hargrave?

Enter Mr. HARGRAVE.

Mr. H. I am here, my Lady—and have juſt heard a tale of ſo atrocious a nature from your ſervants—that I wou'd not, for half my eſtate, ſuch an affair ſhou'd have happen'd in my family.

Lady D. And can you believe the malicious tale?

Mr. H. Indeed I do.

Lady D. Mr. Drummond's arts have then ſucceeded.

Mr. H. *Your* arts have not ſucceeded, my Lady, and you have *no* chance for a huſband now, I believe, unleſs you prevail on George to run off with *you.*

Lady D. Inſolent wretches!—order my chaiſe, I will not ſtay another moment beneath this roof—when perſons of my

rank, thus condefcend to mix with Plebeians—like the Phœnix, which fometimes appears within the ken of common birds,
they are ftared at, jeered and hooted, till they are forced to af-
cend again to their proper region, to efcape the flouts of—
ignorance and envy.   [*Exit.*

  Mr. M. Well faid, a rare fpirit, faith, I fee Ladies of quali-
ty have their privileges too.———[*As Lady D. goes off,* Geo.
fixes his eye on his Father, and points after her.]

  Mr. H. [*catching* George's *hand.*] My dear Boy, I believe
we were wrong here—and I am heartily glad we have efcaped
—but I·fuppofe you'll forget it when I tell you I have no objection to your endeavouring to prevail on this gentleman—

  Geo. Nothing, dear Sir, can prevent my feeling the moft un-
bounded gratitude for the permiffion—now may I hope, Sir—

  Mr. M. Hope, Sir!—Upon my word I don't know what to
fay, you have fomehow contrived to carry matters to fuch
a length—that afking my confent is become a matter of·form. ·.

  Mr. H. Upon my foul, I begin to find out, that in fome
cafes one's children fhould lead.—Come, Sir,—do keep me in
countenance, that I mayn't think I yielded too foon.

  Mr. D. Your confent, Sir, is all we want, to become a
very joyous circle—let us prevail on you to permit your be-
loved Emily to receive the addreffes of my Godfon, and you
will many happy years hence recollect his boldnefs on the
road, as the moft fortunate rencounter of your life : you fhall
come and live amongft us, and we'll reconcile you to your
native country : notwithftanding our ideas of the degeneracy
of the times, we fhall find room enough to act virtuoufly, and
to enjoy in England, more fecurely than in any other country in the world,—the rewards of virtue.

  Mr. M. Sir, I like you—promife me your friendfhip—
and you fhall difpofe of my Niece.

  Mr. D. I accept the condition with pleafure.

  Mr. M. There it is now, this is always the way——perfuaded out of every refolution—a perfect proverb for flexibility.

  Geo. Oh, Sir, permit me———

  Mr. M. Nay, no extacies——Emily diflikes you now
you've got me on your fide. What fay you ? [*to Em.*] don't
you begin to feel your ufual reluctance?

  Em. The proof I have given of my fentiments, Sir, ad-
mits of no difguife—or, if difguife were neceffary, I could
not affume it.

  Geo. Enchanting franknefs ! my heart, my life muft thank
you for this goodnefs. But what fhall I fay to you—[*to
Drummond*] to you, Sir, to whom I already owe more than—

  Mr. D. To me you owe nothing—the heart, George, muft
have fome attachments——·Mine has for many years been

center'd in you——If I have ſtruggled for your happineſs——
'twas to gratify myſelf.

Geo. Oh, Sir! why will you continually give me ſuch
feelings, and yet refuſe them utterance?—Seymour, behold the
happieſt of men!

Sir Cha. May your bliſs, my dear George, be as perma-
nent as 'tis great.—[*To Hargrave*] Allow me, Sir, to ſeize this
propitious moment to aſk your conſent to a ſecond union——
Permit me to entreat Miſs Hargrave for her hand, and I'll
prove George a vain boaſter, when he calls himſelf the happieſt of men.

Har. Why, Sir Charles, you have choſen a very lucky
moment—but there's no moment in which I ſhould not have
heard this requeſt with pleaſure. Why, Harriet——if we may
believe your eyes, you are not very angry with Sir Charles for
this requeſt.

Har. A requeſt, Sir, which gives you ſo much pleaſure
ought not to give your Harriet pain.

Bel. Lord! you look ſo inſulting with your happineſs, and
ſeem to think I make ſuch an aukward figure amongſt you——
but here [*taking a letter from her pocket*]——this informs me
——that a certain perſon——

Geo. Of the name of—Belville—

Bel. Be quiet—— is landed at Dover, and poſting here——
with all the ſaucy confidence our engagements inſpire him
with.

Mr. D. Say you ſo?——Then we'll have the three weddings celebrated on the ſame day.

Bel. Oh mercy!——I won't hear of it——*Love*, one
might manage that perhaps—but *honour*, *obey*,—— 'tis ſtrange
the Ladies had never intereſt enough to get this ungallant
form mended.

Mr. D. The marriage vow, my dear Bella, was wiſely
framed for common apprehenſions—Love teaches a train of
duties that no vow can reach——that refined minds only can
perceive—but which they pay with the moſt delighted attention. You are now entering on this ſtate——may You——
and You [*to Bella, ſignificantly*] and You [*to the audience*]
poſſeſs the bliſsful envied lot of—Married Lovers!

F I N I S.